Willow Water
stories

Jean Husby

Loonfeather Press
Bemidji, Minnesota

Copyrignt © 2003 by Jean Husby
Engravings copyright © 2003 by Scott Husby
All rights reserved
No part of this work may be reproduced in any manner without written permission, except in critical reviews and articles.

Wood engravings by Scott Husby
First printing 2003
Printed in Canada by Hignell Book Printing
ISBN 0-926147-16-1

Acknowledgments

An earlier version of "The Holy Lie" was first published under the title "The Lullaby" in *26 Minnesota Writers*, edited by Monica and Emilio DeGrazia, published by Nodin Press, Minneapolis, Minnesota 1995, and is used by permission.

"Springtime Rebellion" was first published in *Plainswoman*, Volume 5 Numbers 9-10 June-July 1983 in Grand Forks, North Dakota. It was later included in an anthology, *There Lies a Fair Land,* edited by Jon Solensten, published by New Rivers Press, St. Paul, Minnesota 1985.

Loonfeather Press
P.O. Box 1212
Bemidji, Minnesota 56619

This book is dedicated to:

My father, George Vaatveit (1886-1970)
He, by example, made me an avid reader

My mother, Anna Oppegaard Vaatveit (1890-1957)
She taught me Norwegian ways

My sister, Hjordis Vaatveit Dille
She gave me, when I was very young, the idea of becoming a writer

Contents

Introduction   5

Young Mother   7

The Holy Lie   17

Forbidden Fruit   31

Hilde   41

Outsiders   49

About Ingrid   65

Springtime Rebellion   87

Introduction

In northwestern Minnesota there is a small prairie lake, surrounded by willows, that was known, when I was growing up, as Willow Water. It was never Willow Water Lake, just Willow Water. Later, in researching the development of the region, I found an unpublished historical account that went something like this: "There was a small settlement at Willy Water that was soon abandoned as its inhabitants moved to other towns in the area." Willy Water? No, I thought, it must be Willow Water. The name appealed to me and I began to write stories of an imaginary town on its shores and of the people who lived there.

The characters I created are composites of people I have known or heard of, and I gave them traits and behaviors that I have observed over the years. They talk and think and act and feel, revealing flaws as well as virtues.

A farmhouse that I knew intimately in my high school years became the Ingeborg home in "Forbidden Fruit." A second cousin, more than a generation my senior, who lived out her life in northwestern Minnesota, told me stories about people she had known, some of them our relatives, who had died before I was born. From small bits of her information I dreamed up fictional plots and characters and settings. And the story of "Hilde" came from one sentence of a conversation I had with one of my husband's nephews.

In researching the background of my stories, I learned of a fire at Ellis Island that had destroyed some of the records at Castle Garden—information that played a part in "The Holy Lie." The boat "Hekla" was developed from a book I found in the library of Fana Folk School near Bergen, Norway, when we were in that country in 1998. The information about the railroads in western Minnesota and of the brochures that were sent to people in Norway to entice them to emigrate to the midwest are historically accurate.

Local history of this part of northwestern Minnesota is quite well documented and much genealogical research has been done. However, there are few works of fiction, and that is why I was inspired to write the Willow Water stories.

Jean Husby

YOUNG MOTHER

1885

She had been dreaming, a pleasant dream of the green valley in Norway, seeing the clear waters of the Driva flowing along to the fjord. Around her the darkness held noises: whisperings, rustlings, a cough, rhythmic snoring. From beneath the floor came the harsh sounds of the turning screws, the staccato of trembling steel railings and hawsers. Brit, on waking in this alien place was confused and disoriented. She lifted her head to look around. The two-year-old child at her side whimpered, stirred in his sleep and brought her back to the world of reality.

She smoothed the wet hair from her small son's hot, clammy forehead and breathed a lullaby, "*Bya, bya, liten gutt. Bya, bya liten gutt.*" The child settled closer and slept.

Willow Water

Marit, sleeping on the other side of little Arne, kicked the thin partition as she rolled over. Brit hoped her two girls would sleep on so she could go back to the dream and delay her return into steerage, the troubling world of the steamship Hekla's hold.

Her own private world was troubling enough. Arne needed nourishment. She wished she could give the child her breast, but it was more than eight months since she had nursed him and now she had no milk for him. She closed her eyes and thought of the cows in the dale, heard the sound of milk streaming into the pail, SSSSST, ssst, SSSSST, ssssst as she pulled the teats of Varfru. She felt the warmth of the animal as she pressed her head into its side. SSSSST, ssst. The fragrant white liquid filled the pail.

The intrusive present interrupted her reverie. Here her children had no milk; there had been none since they left the farm seven weeks ago. Arne would not eat the grøt she worked so hard to cook. Oh, those dirty, filthy galleys! One day she had steeled herself to stand in line to use the fire. With no milk for the gruel she must use water with the oats. It needed to cook longer but an impatient fellow passenger elbowed her aside and grumbled, "Move on, move on, it's my turn," and then Arne wouldn't eat. The gruel ran down the front of his already soiled shirt. So she had given up on cooking. They were living on flatbrød and cheese and dried meat.

"*Mor*— *Mor!* I have to go." Hilde's round face appeared over the side of the upper bunk.

"Wake Father, Hilde. I cannot move Arne."

"*Far*," Brit heard Hilde plead with Olaf. The chubby four-year-old and her father tumbled out of the bunk. Olaf found the pot and helped the child squat over it. Relieved, she clambered back up to her warm bed.

A shaft of light started to penetrate the darkness of the hold. Brit

Young Mother

and Olaf were fortunate to have been assigned bunks close by the stairway to the deck. At least they were aware of daylight; many others in this dank cavern were not. But daylight brought Brit wholly into the present. She looked around and saw a fellow passenger sitting at the long table that separated this row of bunks from the next one. With elbows on the table, he held his disheveled head in his hands and stared straight ahead. She looked up at the stained canvas of the straw-filled mattress in the upper bunk. Seeing was bad, but smelling was unbearable. Urine, unwashed bodies, dirty clothes, moldy food. She tucked her head down into the quilt. It had been clean from home and still retained a hint of the fresh, pure air of the homeland they were leaving.

Olaf touched her shoulder. "Brit, get up! Today we reach America. We must get ready."

"And what of Arne, Olaf?" There was anguish in her voice. The boy, seeming to hear his name, opened his dull, fever-glazed eyes. Olaf looked away.

"My Arne, little Arne," Brit murmured.

Olaf brushed past the bunk and started up the stairs to the men's outbuilding on the deck above. Arne closed his eyes and his mother held him close. Her desperation mounted. Why could not Olaf do something? The foul water! The moldy food! She began to blame Olaf for all the horrors of this voyage, because her Arne was—she dared not name it, even to herself.

Britha looked older than her twenty-four years. The journey to the fjord, the waiting for a boat to take them down the coast of Norway to Bergen, the sea voyage itself with ever worsening conditions had taken their toll on her. Where was the pretty young woman of seventeen who had married her handsome Olaf? This mother of three small children looked worn and weary. Her reddish-brown hair, dull

Willow Water

and lifeless, had gone unwashed for weeks. She had pulled it back severely from a center part and rolled it into a bun at the nape of her neck for the sake of neatness. Plump and rounded she had been. Now the bone structure of her face had begun to show and the blue eyes were deep-set in dark circles.

In her despair she blamed her husband. He never allowed anyone to be ill. It was as though by being hard about it he could will the child into wellness. He treated animals that way, too. When Frika, the horse, hurt her foot, he hitched her up and made her pull the wagon as though there was not a thing wrong with her. Brit could hear the crack of his whip and hear Olaf shouting, *"Hypp, hypp, kom deg igang for faen!"* When she was with child and suffering with morning sickness he would say, "You are all right, Brit. Don't give in to it." Now with Arne, he was trying not to see the illness of the child. What was she to do? *America!* she thought disdainfully, *I would rather stay poor and live in Norway, in the valley.* Her thoughts smoothed a bit as she allowed herself to remember lovelier times.

Olaf came back and she heard Hilde stirring in the upper bunk. Brit glanced over, looked directly into the eyes of Marit. Her eldest child, only six, lay very still and looked at her mother, then down at Arne. There was sadness in her eyes. *She knows,* thought the mother, as she tousled the child's brown curly hair. "Today we reach America, Marit. Let's get up and have a bite to eat. Then we'll try to make ourselves a little cleaner before we leave the ship."

As the girl crawled over her mother she put her cheek to Brit's and softly touched Arne's damp blonde hair. A sensitive child, Marit. Brit felt a nearness to her firstborn daughter who, unlike her younger sister Hilde, seemed to sense the mood of those around her. Brit's thoughts dwelt on her daughters only momentarily, for her concern was concentrated on the small boy. She gently took her arm from

Young Mother

around Arne and with the other hand covered him as she slid out of the bunk. She straightened the bedding and then began to sort the children's clothing which lay in a crumpled heap at the foot of the bunk. A small shoe dropped to the floor with a thud.

Hilde slid down from above and Olaf started to help her dress. The small girl pushed him away. "I can do buttons," and she did. She handed him her sash. "You can tie this for me, *Far.*"

As he turned her around to do as she asked he spoke to her. "This is an important day, Hilde, one you will remember for the rest of your life." His voice registered pleasure.

Brit could feel the sense of excitement that filled her husband, but she was filled with apprehension. She knew Olaf was looking forward across the miles to the imagined land in the state of Minnesota with certainty that he had made the right decision, to emigrate, to leave the small land holding in Norway in order to have a big farm in this new land. He ignored her apprehension, a pattern of living that would become habitual over the years. She was his wife and she was expected to follow him. At this moment, in the hold of the ship Hekla, on the day of arrival in America, bitterness began to develop within the young woman. She could not have articulated how she felt. It was simply there.

The day was filled with interminable waiting. An undercurrent of unrest, a pervasive fear of the unknown held the Hekla passengers in suspension. Delight at the prospect of reaching the new land surfaced in the children and in those adults who optimistically felt sure everything would turn out just fine.

Olaf's optimism was grounded not only in his belief in the rightness of his decision to emigrate, but also in the fact that he had enough *penger* sewn into his underwear to take advantage of the Homestead Law. Soon he would have 160 acres of fertile farmland under the plow.

Willow Water

As he looked out over the water toward the entry point at Castle Garden he wondered about the cost of the next leg of their journey. He had read all the information he could get his hands on: newspaper accounts, brochures from the ship companies, letters from his cousin already living in Minnesota's Goodhue County. There would be fares to pay when he found out how they would travel. He figured he had enough money to see them settled.

Loaded with belongings, the small family followed other immigrants off the boat, across the dock and into the building where they would be subjected to the inspection they all dreaded. They must qualify for a landing card.

A uniformed official moved them on through the door to the first station where a weary-looking doctor quickly assessed each person's physical condition. Approval for Olaf and the two girls was instantaneous.

Then it was Brit's and Arne's turn. The doctor put his hand to the child's burning cheek. "Your boy has a fever," he told Brit in English.

Brit shook her head in dismay and said in her native tongue, "I don't understand you."

The doctor motioned for her to set the child down. Arne's glazed eyes held the doctor's as his legs collapsed and he slid to the floor. The doctor picked him up and gently placed him in his mother's arms. Then he chalked a white x on the upper sleeve of the boy's jacket and beckoned to a young man, whose job it was to direct people to the next station. Brit searched the line ahead of her for a glimpse of Olaf and the girls but couldn't see them. Mother and child were diverted to a Detention Room. The young man led them to the end of a long pew-like bench and indicated that they should sit down. "You will have to wait here for another physician to make a diagnosis," he explained to the uncomprehending and mute woman. Absorbed with

Young Mother

the child in her arms, she was unaware of others in the room. People came and went. Small groups formed and dissolved and re-formed in her peripheral vision, dreamlike.

Brit did not see Olaf again until he and the girls stood before her. A tall man dressed in the old-country Sunday best of a fellow immigrant followed them.

"Brit, this is Carl Lindquist. He's a Swede. He knows Norwegian and some English and will help us." The man shook hands with Brit across the still bundle she held in her arms. "I have to change my money into American so I can pay for the next fares. Lindquist here will translate for me. We will return as soon as we can."

Brit nodded.

The two girls had seated themselves next to their mother on the hard bench. Now Hilde jumped to the floor and tugged on her father's hand. "I want to go with you." Olaf looked unwilling, but at the child's pleading he gave in and took her.

Time dragged on. Brit sat woodenly, holding the still child. Marit watched as a man with a white x on his sleeve was led through a doorway. She turned around to see a baby who was crying. From time to time she stole glances at her mother and Arne. Finally a woman in white approached holding out her arms for the boy. To the young mother, longing for help, this woman represented expertise, medical authority. Obediently, Brit released him. Mother and daughter were alone together on the long bench. Occasionally Brit would raise her head to look at the clock mounted above a door at the end of the room. Minutes passed, an hour passed. She tried to imagine what was happening to her boy. In her mind she saw a doctor bending over the child. Then, her thoughts drifted to their home in Norway. She had glimpses of little Arne toddling along, carrying a stick, "helping" her drive Varfru into the stable, saw him toss stones into the swiftly flowing river.

13

Willow Water

The minutes dragged on. Marit dropped down on the bench and snuggled against her mother's body. Her eyes kept falling shut and soon she slept. Brit, tired beyond sleep, tired beyond thought, sat there, unmoving.

The two men and Hilde returned. Olaf could not conceal his excitement. "We have booked passage up the Hudson River and as soon as Arne is returned to us we will leave Castle Garden." The children, captivated by their unusually animated father, jumped down from the bench and stood before him. Brit sat very still and looked at him. "A map was spread out before us," he said, "and Carl and another fellow located Minnesota—to determine which way we should go to get there."

Just then the nurse who had taken Arne approached the group, empty-handed. She touched the Swede's arm and started speaking very slowly and distinctly, "You must tell the parents that Arne is to be taken to a hospital in a place called Ward's Island in the East River."

Lindquist carefully relayed the information to Olaf.

"Do we go there, too?" Olaf wanted to know.

Lindquist translated his question into English for the nurse.

"No, they must wait here at Castle Garden. They can't stay in the Detention Room but they can stay in the Waiting Room, even sleep on the benches there. Perhaps tomorrow," Lindquist translated.

"But we have our tickets for the next boat. What about that?" There was anguish in Olaf's voice.

The nurse drew Lindquist aside. "The boy is dying, you know. It would be best if you could get them to accept that. There is no way he can be saved."

Lindquist stood there for a few moments, then slowly returned to the family. In his unhappiness at the prospect of relaying this information, he reverted to his native Swedish, *"Barnet ligger för döden"* which means, "The child is before (or near) death." Brit understood

Young Mother

Carl's Swedish words, similar to her native Norwegian. "Near death! Near death!" Brit's words were a cry. She pulled on Olaf. "I want my boy. Bring him to me!" It was a command. "We will take him with us." She faced him square on.

"A dying child? Brit, we cannot do that." Olaf looked down at his hands.

"Find us a room, Olaf, and bring me my boy. I need to feed him."

Carl Lindquist, ordinarily a mild-mannered man, took hold of the nurse's arm and vehemently insisted, "I must talk to the doctor myself. This is not right. You must let me speak to the doctor."

She stood there for a few moments and then agreed. "All right. Come with me." Lindquist followed her and they disappeared through a door.

Brit continued to plead with her husband, kept on pleading into his silence. Marit rubbed tears from her eyes. Hilde fidgeted. "Olaf, Olaf, do something! Do not just stand there. Tell them we will not leave our boy."

The door opened and the Swede returned alone. He approached the group very slowly, and then pulled Olaf off away from the others. His eyes were sad as he spoke. "Olaf Aasen, you must go. The doctor says it is the only way. The child will not last the night."

Brit rose and hurried to the two men, "Near death—near death—not dead—there is hope. Olaf we must stay and get Arne, find a house, here—work—here. I will take care of my boy and he will get well again and we will return to Norway." Olaf stood there with his arms at his side. "Do not be this way Olaf! Do not be so hard." Olaf took a deep breath and closed his eyes. "Arne is your son Olaf, your only son! We cannot leave Arne."

"Come Brit, come." Olaf put his arm around the distraught woman and propelled her out of the Detention Room with Marit and Hilde clinging to their parents' clothing. Lindquist stood very still and watched as they walked the length of the room toward the door.

THE HOLY LIE

1896

Marit knew that her father never regretted his decision to emigrate from Norway. In fact, he felt the hand of his Lutheran God directing every aspect of his life. Here in western Minnesota the prairie sod asked only to be turned and worked, whereas the rocky, mountainous land of Norway had battled him all the way. Each year the fertile loam of his quarter section of land yielded bigger and better crops of oats, barley and flax. A fine herd of Holsteins grazed along the willow-lined river. He had built a barn and replaced the crude log cabin with a new white clapboard house.

Marit, at seventeen, was proud of her father, his farm, and the new house. Her mother who (it seemed to Marit) was still yearning for her old home in Norway had taken no interest in the planning. Marit gradually took Brit's place; helped make all sorts of decisions such as room size, the location of doors and windows, even the choice of wood for the mantelpiece. In one instance only did Brit rouse herself to make a decision. She chose wallpaper for the parlor, a pattern of big red roses. Marit hated those roses. Yet the very fact that Brit had asserted herself to voice a preference in the matter gave Marit hope that her mother would become less distanced from all that was taking place around her, and so she said nothing.

In their life on the farm the positions of Marit and fifteen-year-old Hilde were well defined. An unspoken law decreed that Hilde assume the place of the son Olaf had lost. She worked the farm with her father, was as adept as he at driving their team of work horses to plow, harrow, disc, rake and plant. In 1896 an early spring woke the land with sunny days and warm showers, and by mid-June Hilde and Olaf were cutting the sweet-smelling hay.

As was the custom in Norway, so it was in Minnesota; the women milked the cows. Twice daily Brit and Hilde drove the lumbering creatures into the barn for milking. Marit was never asked to help with this ritual. She was expected to stay inside to do the housework, to cook and wash and clean.

Her household tasks gave her much time with her mother and could have produced a closeness between the two, but they did not. Brit kept her own counsel. Contained within herself, she reached out to no one, not to Olaf nor Marit nor Hilde.

Marit remembered times, before the long voyage, when her young mother, with a twinkle in her clear blue eyes, laughed with her children, told them stories, even sang and danced around with them. Now those light blue eyes were dull. She went about her daily work on the farm, doing what was required of her, without any attempt to make

The Holy Lie

life pleasant or joyful for the family or herself. She seemed indifferent to what went on about her. Yet she was never idle. It was as if work was the panacea for all that troubled her. A compulsive need to use her hands constantly manifested itself. Wherever she went, if she was not carrying pails of feed for the chickens, or produce from the garden, or buckets of milk, Brit would remove her knitting from a large pocket in her apron and knit as she walked. She made scarves, mittens and sweaters in drab grays and tans. The neighbors joked about her, speculated that she even knit underwear for Olaf. The sound of her knitting needles became synonymous with the woman, Britha.

One day in Johansson's General Store, as Marit was bent over the thread cabinet trying to find the right shade of blue to match a swatch of dress fabric, she overheard Nora Espeseth and two other farm women gossiping. They were unaware of the girl, hidden by a pile of unopened bolts of cloth stacked on a table. They used the Norwegian word *gamle* to describe a woman as an old-country person, one who is unable or unwilling to become American.

"Olaf needs a son," Nora stated. "Hilde works with him like a man, but he should have a son."

They're talking about Mor, Marit realized.

"It must be eleven, twelve years now since they came here," Mrs. Carlson added, "and no more children in all that time." She herself had nine. "How does Britha do it?"

The third woman (Marit couldn't see who was talking) surmised, "One of these days Olaf will look around for a willing woman. It's a wonder he hasn't already."

Marit peeked around the stacks of fabric to see the gossipers.

"Losing that child when they came to this country has affected her." Nora pointed to her head.

Marit suddenly felt the anguished despair her mother must have

19

Willow Water

felt that day when her desperately ill brother, Arne, had been taken from them at the Port of Entry. That day, at the age of 6, she had suffered with her mother in the bewilderment of what was happening. Now, she understood everything the women were saying. From that time on Marit saw her mother in a different light and her concern deepened.

Several weeks later she and Hilde came home from school earlier than usual. Their farm was on the edge of town, a mile and a half from the school. In the snowy winter they followed the wagon road, while spring and fall offered a shortcut around the fields and through the pasture to their house. On this particular spring day Hilde dallied by the last place in town to watch old Mr. Harstad dig a drainage ditch at the side of the road, but Marit hurried along on the path toward home. When she reached the farmhouse she quietly let herself in, not really knowing why she was being so quiet.

From her parents' room came faint strains of music. Marit was puzzled. Could Mor be singing? Still wearing her wraps, her schoolbooks under her arm, she moved slowly, silently down the hallway. Approaching the open door, she stopped, astounded. Her mother, who no longer sang, was singing. *"Bya, bya, liten gutt."* Sitting in her rocking chair in front of a window, she was softly crooning the lullaby to a bundle of clothes she cradled tenderly in her arms. *"Bya, bya, liten gutt,"* over and over and then humming on and on. She rocked back and forth, moving with the tune. Marit melted deeper into the hall. Into her consciousness flooded memories of the hold on the ship Hekla. She was listening to the sounds of her mother trying to soothe Arne. She could smell the stinking hold, hear the gratings and groanings of the ship as she lay against the rough wall on the lower bunk. She remembered crawling across Mor and Arne and looking into the glazed eyes of the whimpering child. *"Bya, bya, liten gutt."* The rocking mother, aware of nothing but the "child" in her arms, sang on and on.

The Holy Lie

The words of the local woman came to Marit with a rush. "Losing that child has affected her." Was she right? Was Mor's mind affected? Was she still grieving for Arne? And is it possible Arne is still alive, that he didn't die that day at Castle Garden? Softly Marit slipped into the kitchen and, without removing her coat, sat down at the oilcloth-covered table. She gazed blindly out the window and heard her mother's pleading voice, those many years ago, when they had to leave Arne at Castle Garden. "Please, Olaf, please let us stay here and take care of Arne. I must feed him." And then she heard the silence of her father.

From that moment on she began to watch her mother more closely, to see her more clearly, to feel a need to protect her. The impulse to help her mother was slowly shaping Marit's life.

Again and again she encouraged her mother to learn English. Patiently, she let Britha know that she understood that in living here in Willow Water there was no urgent need to learn the new language; half the inhabitants were Norwegians who spoke their native tongue. "But these immigrants want to become American," she explained carefully. "Do you not want to become American?" Brit did not answer. Marit tried to make fun of it, this language thing, by noting that even the *Setesdalen* were losing their accents. Brit did not laugh. Marit told herself not to be so impatient, reminded herself that she had teachers at school to help her while Brit had no one except her family. "This is a *cup,* Mother. This is a *plate.* We are going to *church.*" Brit simply ignored her, pulled out her knitting and let the clack, clack of the needles take over.

Marit and Hilde did indeed go to church and in English. The Lutheran Church itself was divided by language, offering one service a week in Norwegian, one in English. Olaf yearned to go to the English service with his daughters, for he had made steady progress in learning his adopted tongue, but in this matter he must consider the wishes of his wife. His religion taught that one must do nothing to cause another to lose faith. If he did not take Britha to church she would quit going and he would have sinned. Anticipated guilt dictated his actions. So, Brit and Olaf continued worshipping with a dwindling group of old-country parishioners clinging to familiar ways. Olaf, with his erect bearing (he had served two years in the Army of Norway), would walk up the center aisle, his right hand on the elbow of his shawl-clad wife. They would seat themselves in the fifth pew from the front of the pulpit in order to look directly at Reverend Langemoe.

The community of Willow Water looked up to the Reverend Langemoe. He was articulate, well-read, the best-educated man in town. They called him *Reverend*, not the more informal *Pastor*. A tall man, big-boned and with a commanding presence, he exuded authority. There was something aristocratic about him that demanded deference. Yet the people liked him for his trustworthiness, and they knew he cared about them.

Marit's clear soprano voice found her a place in the church choir, and Hilde, not wanting to sit alone in church, joined too. In early spring of 1895 Reverend Langemoe had asked Marit to lead a children's choir. Someone was needed to teach the young ones to sing the hymns in English. He offered, as her helper and organist, his daughter Livia, and so began a friendship that was to last a lifetime. The two girls would spend hours together, Liv informally teaching her friend to play the organ. When winter came, the coldness of the church nave drove them to the parsonage where they continued their music together at the Langemoe's piano.

Marit envied her friend that piano, coveted it. She asked her father if there were any possibility they might buy one for their house. "Perhaps, sometime," was his half-yes reply. Indeed, Olaf liked the idea of being rich enough to own a musical instrument. Marit's musical

The Holy Lie

talent came from him, of this he was sure. If it were not for Brit, he would offer his deep bass voice to the choir. Yes, some day he would buy a piano. As for Marit, she spent more and more of her time at the parsonage.

On a blustery day in March the two girls were playing duets when Liv's father entered the room, ostensibly searching for a notebook. Instead of leaving when he could not find it, he folded himself down into a chair to watch and listen. The girls stopped playing and looked at him. "Yes, Father?" Liv questioned.

He rose and approached the piano. "Marit, I've been thinking about your family." He leaned an arm across the corner of the piano top. "What can we do to get your mother to be part of the congregation?"

Marit's face flushed.

"She comes only to the Norwegian services with your father," he continued. "She doesn't have anything to do with any of the ladies. She should be coming to the women's meeting." He paused. "Why doesn't she come?"

"She doesn't speak English." Marit stated what they both knew.

"Some of the women would speak to her in Norwegian."

"But the program is in English, Reverend Langemoe."

"Yes, that's true. Still, we must do something to try to get her to come."

"I can try," the girl answered, but added honestly, "I don't think she will."

Over the next few weeks variations of this same conversation took place between the clergyman and Marit. Then, one day, when Liv was not in the room, Marit braved the situation and spoke her thoughts to this man she had learned to know and trust. "I think Mor is very unhappy. I found her singing one day." She went on to tell him about the day she found her mother holding the bundle of clothes, rocking and singing the lullaby. "I think if my mother could find out what happened to Arne at Castle Garden, she would be happier. I really think she believes that he is out there somewhere. But it is so strange. She thinks of him as a baby. He would be thirteen years old by now." She was silent for a while and then added, "I think she is not sure that he died that day and it keeps her unhappy."

Although Langemoe knew the story of the child left at the Port of Entry, the idea that they had not tried to find out about him had not occurred to him. Now he realized how deeply the girl had considered her mother. He sat for a few minutes looking out the window at the yellow-green of the early spring leaves. He must verify what he suspected and asked, "Has your father tried to find out what happened?"

Marit shook her head. She looked at her hands and waited for him to speak.

"It wouldn't hurt to try to find out for sure. Maybe we should try." He tapped one foot and continued to look at the spring landscape. "I'm going to Crookston next week. I'll make inquiries about how to go about it." He turned to face Marit. "And then we shall speak to your father."

He made the three-day trip to Crookston, the County Seat. The county attorney told him to write to the Immigration Service in Washington, D.C.

On his return to Willow Water, the conscientious minister suggested again to Marit that they should involve her father in this endeavor. She hesitated and then refused, fearing he might put a stop to the process.

The clergyman crafted a letter. "I am writing on behalf of a parishioner, Miss Marit Aasen." He stated the problem. "She would like to know if your records show that her brother, Arne Aasen, then aged two years, died at Castle Garden, the New York Port of Entry, on May 15, 1885." He went on to give the authorities all the information

The Holy Lie

Marit could give him of the family's departure from Norway and arrival in the United States.

Then, once more he encouraged Marit to tell her parents what they had done, that the letter had been written. Only after the letter had been posted did Marit follow his advice and tell them.

With uncharacteristic excitement Brit asked, "When will we hear? Will the government write to you, a girl of seventeen? How long will it take? It was good of Reverend Langemoe to help you."

"Marit, you shouldn't bother the reverend with our troubles." Olaf's voice was gruff. "I am disappointed in you." His voice rose. "You should not have done it! I don't like it at all!" He slammed the door as he stormed out of the kitchen.

No more was said of the matter, although it hovered in all their minds. Marit attempted to pray, but could not. For what should she pray? *Do I want to know Arne is living out there somewhere, no one knows where? That would be worse than knowing he is dead. What is Mor thinking?* Brit seemed to Marit to be more unapproachable than ever. *Perhaps she thinks talking about it would not please Father—and she is right there,* Marit reasoned with herself. *Father doesn't want other people consulted about matters that he thinks should stay in the family, and he hates speculation about anything.* Weeks passed. Her hopes of getting definite information, whatever that might be, began to fade. *Perhaps Far was right and she should not have troubled Reverend Langemoe. Perhaps it was better not to know.*

Fall moved closer to winter. The girls concentrated on their studies.

On a crisp, cold Friday in November, Liv approached Marit at school to give her a message. Her father would like to talk to her "at his study in the church tomorrow morning."

"At the church?" Marit questioned this unusual request.

"That's what he asked me to tell you," Liv replied matter-of-factly.

Willow Water

"I don't know why."

The minister's study at the Norwegian Lutheran Church was in front of the nave, a small room off to the right side of the ornate wooden Gothic altar. To get there, one must go through the wide-open worship space. On that afternoon in November a disquieting sense of foreboding surrounded the girl as she walked quietly over the wooden floorboards through the cold, empty room, up the steps and along the altar rail. She looked up at the familiar painting on the altar wall of Christ leaving the tomb, the two Roman soldiers lying at either side of an opening to a cave, holding their shields before their eyes. The rich brown of the soldier's tunics, their hard helmets, and Christ all white and shining. She knocked at the door.

"Come in."

The man sitting behind his desk, in his black suit and white clerical collar was The Minister, not her friend's father. Marit felt awe in the presence of the official clergy. She stood there.

"Please be seated, Marit." Reverend Langemoe pushed back his chair a few inches, opened his top desk drawer and removed a long, important-looking envelope which he placed in front of him on his desk. "The Immigration Service answered our letter." He put on his metal-rimmed glasses and looked at Marit. She sat forward on her chair. Her gray mittens fell to the floor. The minister's serious tone stifled the smile that had started to appear on her young face. "It is not what we were hoping for." He took the letter out of its envelope and spread it on the desk before him. "Now, Marit, God's ways are not our ways. You know that. He works in mysterious ways." He went on in this vein while Marit waited. Finally he said, "I will read part of it to you. He lifted the white paper up in front of him. "Here it says, 'I regret to inform you that I can be of no help in verifying the death of Arne Aasen. The immigrant records were moved from Castle Garden

The Holy Lie

to the new facility on Ellis Island. Last year there was a fire at Ellis Island and all the records for the Port of New York for the years from 1855 to 1890 were destroyed.' " Reverend Langemoe took off his glasses, laid them alongside the letter, then raised his eyes to search the face of the girl in front of him. A deep silence enveloped the two.

"How will I tell Mor and Father?" Marit's question was anguished.

"You . . ." and she considered the competent authoritarian figure before her. "No, I should tell them. Father would not . . ." and her voice trailed off, "but Mor . . ."

"You will find a way, Marit. The Lord will help you. You must pray for guidance." He sat there for a minute, then picked up the letter, folded it and slipped it back into the envelope. He handed it to her across the desk. "Here, take the letter with you and show it to your father. Shall we have a word of prayer together?"

Marit's footsteps dragged as she walked the path around the field toward home. She picked up a stick and struck dry leaves from the grasses and low-lying plants as she walked, not in anger, but rather giving a rhythm to her thoughts. When she reached the pasture she threw down the stick and stopped for a while before letting herself through the fence gate. Her smooth, seventeen-year-old forehead was furrowed. Suddenly, her chin jutted out and she pursed her lips as if saying to herself, "Well, that's what I have to do." Kicking some pebbles with the toe of her high-topped shoe, she walked on with an air of determination.

The noon meal was always a hearty one on the farm and the family took time to eat it. On this Saturday in November the meal seemed interminable to Marit, yet she wanted to lengthen it. When the family had finished the last morsel of their bread pudding, she pulled the letter from her pocket.

"You heard from the Immigration Service," Olaf stated in surprise.

Willow Water

Brit became agitated. "Tell me, tell me." She plucked at her daughter's shoulder.

Hilde jumped up to stand behind Marit. "Well, read it, Marit. Read it."

"You have to sit down, Hilde." Marit became quite formal. "I will tell you, in Norwegian for Mor's sake, what it says." She took a deep breath, glanced once at her father, then looking directly into her mother's eyes began slowly. "Mor, the letter says that Arne died that day at Castle Garden." She paused. "There was a Lutheran chaplain there to serve all the Scandinavian immigrants. He said prayers over Arne when they buried him." Marit held the letter in her lap. They all sat still as if frozen in position. "That's all the letter says," Marit concluded limply.

Britha said nothing. She pushed back her chair and rose from the table, took off her big-pocketed apron and hung it on a hook on the wall, put on her heavy gray sweater that hung there. The family watched as she opened the door to the back porch. They heard the slam of the outside door as Brit let herself out into the cool November air. From where he sat Olaf could see his wife as she veered off the road and headed across the meadow in the direction of the willows and the river. Marit longed for her father to go after her, to speak to her, touch her, but she knew he would not.

Olaf picked up his battered brown felt hat from the floor where he had dropped it before the meal and pushed back his chair. It grated on the floor. "Hilde, come. We have work to do."

Solemnly Marit handed her father the letter. He folded it in half and palmed it into his back pocket without looking at it.

FORBIDDEN FRUIT
1913

I'd have given anything to go to one of the Nygaard dances. The sound of fiddle music, laughter and singing drifted across the water as I knelt down in front of my wide open bedroom window to listen. I could picture myself there twirling around the floor with Nordahl as Edward and Roy filled the night air with their lively music. But I could only dream on that midsummer's night. I rested my arm on the windowsill to cushion my head and closed my eyes, listening.

Nordahl had said, "We're dancing on Saturday night. Why don't you walk over?" Our farm, the Berg farm, was across the lake from the Nygaard place. I knew before asking that Ma and Pa would not hear of it. And since Nordahl's brother had been in a fight and been thrown in jail there was no use asking, no use at all. Pa had said, "Good-for-nothing Nygaards! I knew something like this would happen."

Those dances in the Nygaard house—Guri told me what fun they were. She went to all of them with her family.

"Pa says there's drinking—is there?" I asked her.

"There's home brew down in the granary for the old men. Pa goes down and has a glass. What's so bad about that, Thea?" Everyone, including my friend Guri, called me *Tee-ah* in those days, Norwegian. Now I'm *Thea*, American.

"You know how Ma and Pa are, Guri. No drinking, no dancing, especially no drinking."

"These dances are family affairs, Thea. We all bring food and the Nygaards make coffee—and nectar for the kids. We all dance, even Ingeborg." Ingeborg was Edward's wife, mother of Nordahl and Roy, Karen, Calma, Ferd and four more children. To say that Ingeborg danced is to say a pregnant woman danced, for it seemed she was always with child.

In September of that year, the fall of 1913, my uncle and aunt, who lived over by Ada, invited Pa and Ma to drive over for some pheasant hunting. They were to leave on a Friday and wanted me to skip school that day and go with them, but I didn't want to go—I was 17 years old and a senior in high school and couldn't miss a day of my last year. I convinced them to go without me. My brother Bjorn went with them; he, like Pa, wanted to hunt pheasants. My older brother Ole offered to stay home. Someone had to do the chores—milk the cows, feed the chickens and the pigs. Ole would do the chores—and watch over me, I was sure.

Guri, my best friend, when she found out they were going, asked me to come over and stay with her on Saturday night. Ma liked Guri's

Forbidden Fruit

mother and gave her permission, without really thinking about it. She didn't know on that Saturday night there was to be a dance at the Nygaard's.

Guri told Nordahl our plans—that I was going to stay with her on Saturday night and Nordahl told Guri to be sure to come to the dance and bring me with her. He was a year out of high school by then, working in Willow Water at the lumber yard, bringing home part of his paycheck to help pay for adding another room to the Nygaard house. He loved to dance, even did a *Halling,* that one-man Norwegian folk dance from the old country. I hadn't seen him do it, but Guri told me he was really good at it.

"You will go to the dance with us, won't you, Thea?"

"If Pa and Ma find out I'll be punished."

"How?"

"Oh, Ma is not very hard on us, but Pa might have some different ideas; maybe I'll have to slop the pigs for a week, two or three weeks if Pa has his say. Ma? Well, she might make me scrub the knees of the overalls on the scrub board for . . ."

"Would it be worth it to you? Guri looked directly at me.

I didn't have to think at all. "Yes, Let's go."

We clasped hands and skipped around like little five-or six-year-old girls.

On Friday my parents were off in our wagon, Pa driving, Ma beside him, Bjorn in the back with Jake, our Labrador retriever.

That night Ole and I did the chores together. We got to talking about the Nygaards as we milked the cows.

"You know, Thea, Pa thinks Edward Nygaard is the poorest farmer in the whole county. He came to Minnesota with enough money to buy the farm, but no experience at farming. Did you know, Thea, that Edward's family were landowners in Ringerike? They had a lot of forested land and made their living off the trees. They had a mill.

"Then why did Ingeborg and Edward come here to farm?" I wanted to know.

"Knute tells me it's because Edward wanted to marry Ingeborg—she was a maid on their estate—not one of them, landowners. Edward's mother wouldn't have him marry the girl, just wouldn't hear of it, made life miserable for Edward, fired Ingeborg—so they emigrated to the United States. Knute says Edward's father knew what they were planning to do. He was more reasonable than the mother and gave Edward money for the trip, steerage—he wasn't very generous. So they ran off together. Edward just doesn't know how to farm."

"But he knows how to play the violin," I added.

"Don't think I don't know what you're going to do tomorrow night, Thea." Ole was pouring milk from his pail into the big milk can.

"And what are you going to do about it?" I asked, holding my breath.

"Nothing."

Ole has always been my friend.

"That fancy horse and buggy of Ingeborg's—Pa says they should have spent their money for all the things they needed, not for luxuries." We both laughed. Ingeborg's elegant black buggy and sleek black horse had been the talk, not only of the farmers and their wives, but also of the whole town of Willow Water. And not all kindly. She'd had it for years by the time we were talking about it, but people still made fun of poor pregnant Ingeborg and her fancy carriage.

"Ole, why don't you walk over to Nygaard's on Saturday night? You don't need to be invited, anybody can go."

"Thea, you know I can't dance."

"Guri and I will teach you. It would be fun. C'mon Ole!"

Guri had taught me. We'd go upstairs in their barn, in the

Forbidden Fruit

haymow, clear off some floor space. She would hum the tunes. She taught me to waltz and polka and do the schottishe. It was such fun—and now I had a chance to really dance with real music. I could hardly wait.

Ole wouldn't go. He was shy about it.

What to wear? Guri and I went through my wardrobe. She is a blonde and planned to wear her favorite blue dress. We decided that since my hair is kind of brownish-red and I look great in certain shades of green, I would wear my green wool. It could be quite cool on a September night. I shouldn't be too warm. I took along a narrow gold ribbon to tie back my long hair.

Saturday was a beautiful autumn day. As we piled into Tormundson's wagon that evening yellow leaves were falling all around us, the sun going down in the west. Guri's father drove, with her mother beside him holding a huge wrapped plate of open-faced sandwiches on her lap. We sat in the back with Guri's two younger brothers, our legs hanging down over the back of the wagon, for the short ride to the Nygaard place.

The lake on the Nygaard farm takes up about a quarter of their 160 acres. Pa couldn't understand why Edward bought land with all that water on it. He considered it wasted. Our farm was all tillable land with most of it cleared and planted to crops. Of course we had pasture land for our herd of Jerseys. That was another thing. Pa thought Edward should have more cows, not only for milk, but also for manure to spread on his fields. I think, now, that the lake, in Edward's mind, was part of the reason he was attracted to the land—for its beauty. And it was useful—a drinking place for his animals and for making ice in the winter; he even let Pa cut ice there, so Pa shouldn't have been so critical. Of course we weren't thinking about any of this that Saturday night. We noticed the wild rose bushes covered with red hips, the graceful willows hanging over the lake. What happiness! What expectations!

Mr. Tormundson drove down by the barn to leave the wagon and horses with the other rigs already there. We piled out and started to walk up the hill toward the house. When I saw the number of rigs and single horses tied up down there I asked Guri, "Is there room in the house for all these people?"

"They always move out the furniture to the east side of the house. With Roy and Nordahl and Ferd—plenty of help to move what they have."

One thing my mother disapproved of was Ingeborg's housekeeping. I can't imagine my mother letting anyone move all our furniture out into the yard for any reason. Ingeborg didn't care. She was an indifferent housekeeper. The older daughters did the housework. In fact, Karen told me many years later that she still dreamt about scrubbing those unfinished wooden floors. She cared. But if Ingeborg had cared there would have been no dances in their house. Which is better?

The kitchen door stood wide open. We entered there. Mrs. Tormundson made room on the already-covered table for her plate of sandwiches. One of the neighbor women was adding the usual ground coffee and egg mixture to boiling water in the huge coffeepot on the wood stove. The smell made me think of Ladies Aid at the Lutheran Church. Roy was playing a tune and people were dancing as we moved into the big room, their all-purpose room where the family ate and spent most of their time. Children were sitting on the steps of a stairway leading to the upstairs bedrooms, watching what was going on below them.

Edward, taking his violin from the case, put it down and walked over to greet us. He was a slender man, not tall, his dark brown hair

Forbidden Fruit

sort of curly, with kind eyes. He greeted me by name and then shook hands with the Tormundsons. I liked him immediately. "You'll have to throw your wraps in the pile in the next room," he told us. We made our way around the dancers to rid ourselves of our sweaters and jackets and Mrs. Tormundson's shawl.

Ingeborg was seated in one corner of the room. There were other women with her. She was nursing her baby. *"Velkommen!"* she called out in Norwegian, as she lifted her right hand in greeting. Ingeborg had grown fatter with the birth of each child until it was impossible to tell if she was pregnant or not. She was a pleasant woman, uncomplicated. I could imagine that when she and Edward came to the United States and she was very young she must have been pleasantly plump and quite pretty. I could see her as a maid in the Nygaard household in Norway enticing Edward, yes.

Guri and I joined the dances. She had told me we could dance with everyone. I could dance with her or another girl or one of the boys or the parents or even one of the children. We joined right in.

Guri and I danced together, mixing in with the other couples. Then a friend from high school asked me for the next dance, a polka. He was a good dancer and it was such fun.

Guri's eleven-year-old brother Harald and I galloped around the room for the next piece. As we passed the doorway to the kitchen a man I knew only slightly stumbled through. He pointed to me and in a loud, grumbly voice said, "Hey girlie, com-ere, com-ere." He began making crude remarks to the other women as they danced by. "He's drunk," my young partner whispered. Ferd appeared next to the drunken man and urged him out into the kitchen. I was dismayed—Pa was right, there was some drinking going on. I thought *Guri would say, 'So what?'* I forgot the drunk, went on galloping around with Harald.

Ferd and I did the schottische together. *Deedy deedy dum dum/ deedy deedy dum dum/dee deedy dum dum/dee deedy dum dum*—in my head I sang the tune as Guri had done when she taught me. The line danced through the door into the next room where we'd left our wraps, circled around the open space in there and then back into the big room. Nordahl did this one with Guri. I wished he had asked me, but Ferd was a good partner.

"How about finding something to eat?" Ferdinand led me into the kitchen and Guri and Nordahl followed us. Mrs. Tormundson's sandwiches were all gone. We stood around drinking coffee. There were lots of cookies and cakes.

The room was full to overflowing with men and women eating and talking. Children snatched cookies and ran out into the cool night air, laughing and calling to each other.

Edward and Roy had been making the music together. Now it was time for the father to take a break and he joined other men at the food table. There was easy conversation about the harvest, the coming winter.

We young ones again joined the dancers. Time flew by. I danced all night, never sat one out. The fun would soon be over. Guri took my hand. "The last dance of the night is the *Bryllupsvalsen*. It's a wedding dance from Ringerike." As she told me this Edward and Roy held their bows at the ready. Nordahl appeared at my side. "This one is for me, Thea?"

Oh yes, yes, at last. I smiled at him as he danced me off into the middle of the room. The first part of this music I had never heard, was a simple waltz. Then there was a kind of fast part, then a beautiful slower waltz. Nordahl was the best of dancers. When the music slowed he danced me right out the open front door onto the porch. The full moon was shining on the lake and a cool breeze was blowing.

Forbidden Fruit

And then—he kissed me on the lips, not missing a step, and danced us back into the warm room. As we came through the door I saw two little girls sitting halfway up the stairway. They were watching us, holding their fists in front of their mouths, heads together and giggling. We laughed, and went on enjoying the music and the movement.

I floated through the rest of the night, through the ride back to the Tormundson farm under the starlit sky, feeling happy, not minding the teasing of Guri's brothers—they had seen us, too.

We were getting ready for bed in Guri's room when she brought me back to reality. "Do you think you will be punished?"

"Who cares!" I used her expression.

We settled into Guri's comfortable bed. She gave me the window side. We were quiet, happy-tired. I hugged myself and began to try it out on myself. I wanted to hear how it sounded. Mrs. Nordahl Nygaard, Mrs. Nordahl Nygaard, Mrs. Nordahl—it sounded musical to my inner ear. I drifted off to sleep.

Me, Mrs. Nordahl Nygaard? No. In September of 1916 Nordahl and Guri were married.

Hilde

1915

"I just won't have it, not in this house!" Hilde stormed into the kitchen and set down the pail of warm milk she was carrying.

Marit, standing at the wood range, lifted a dripping wooden spoon out of the bubbling applesauce, grabbed a dishcloth to hold under it and turned toward her angry sister.

Hilde raced on with her tirade. "Sigurd is down there by the barn vomiting—vomiting from too much drink. Our eighteen-year-old brother a common drunkard! I won't have it, you hear me?" She yanked off her scarf and jacket and flung them on a chair, ignoring the pegs above.

Their mother scurried into the kitchen still holding the sock she was darning. "Hilde, Hilde, what is wrong?" Her question was put in

Norwegian and from this point on the sisters lapsed into their mother's native tongue.

"*Mor*, did you hear Sigurd come home this morning?" Hilde confronted her mother.

"Yah, yah—"

"And you heard him stumbling around?"

Brit nodded.

Hilde approached her sister like an interrogating lawyer. "And you, Marit? You heard him, too?"

"I went down to close doors and helped him up the stairs."

"Drunk, wasn't he?" Hilde moved closer to her sister, almost touching her.

"He was drunk all right." Marit turned to the stove and busied herself with her stirring.

"Now we will do something! This cannot go on! We cannot stand for it! The saloons have to go!" Hilde began jabbing her right fist into her left hand. "We must do something!" She tramped from one side of the kitchen to the other.

Hilde had been "doing something" about the problem of drinking in the village for years—but always it had been because of those others out there, "the weak-kneed men of Willow Water who need their alcohol to keep them going." Although she had given quality leadership to the local Woman's Christian Temperance Union, she had been doing it from above, looking down from a moral height. Now, in her own family!

Hilde, at 34, was the one registered nurse in town besides Dr. Hillestad's wife. She had seen men in delirium tremens, women beaten by alcoholic husbands. Her medical experiences had left her with a zealous dedication to the cause of the W.C.T.U. At first she had recruited members in a somewhat ladylike fashion, but gradually her

Hilde

recruitment methods took on an edge. She became an agitator. When trying to convince women to join she did not hesitate to draw detailed verbal pictures of her experiences with alcoholics and to predict what would happen if alcohol consumption in Willow Water were not curtailed. She commanded the women who joined her to urge their friends and relatives to sign a pledge of total abstinence. Hilde herself used coercive tactics to get people to sign that sheet of paper. Some signed it just to get rid of her, with no intention of abstaining from the occasional glass of wine or snort of whiskey.

The people of the town who had been helped in some way by Hilde's compassionate nursing spoke well of her. Her tender, loving care of the elderly endeared her to their families. Others found her manner bullying, her language harsh, her religious zeal excessive, and thought her an overbearing bore. Most of the Willow Water folks, as was their easy habit, laughed when she overdid something and accepted her as a useful part of the community.

In 1915 ten women from the Willow Water area wore the white ribbon, badge of their membership in the WCTU. Some of them tried to direct the group to other (safer) causes espoused by the WCTU, such as better nutrition or better schools, but Hilde kept them centered on what was for her, as leader of the organization, their reason for being—the battle against alcohol. At times, carried away by her zeal and wanting to be more dramatic in her presentation she would refer to all alcohol as "Demon Rum," although little or no rum was actually consumed in the village.

That night when Sigurd came home drunk, the WCTU cause took on a personal dimension for Hilde. She was going to get rid of the three saloons on the downtown street, one way or another.

She called a meeting of the organization.

Ordinarily they met in the Lutheran Church, but this time she convinced Stella Rude to have it in her house. Stella was almost as dedicated as Hilde, for her father had died of acute alcoholism at an early age. Now, when Hilde was faced with her own brother's "deviant" behavior, she enlisted the support of Stella, although she didn't tell her friend what she had in mind. She saved that for the gathering.

On the day of the meeting Stella, dressed in her best flowered housedress, welcomed the women into her cozy parlor. Hilde had strongly suggested that she dispense with the usual opening coffee so the group could get right down to business.

Never one to allow meetings to be delayed by purposeless chatter, Hilde had developed the habit of arriving on the hour and immediately pounding her gavel for order. This day was no exception. She asked the secretary to read the minutes of the last meeting. The treasurer gave her report. There was a check on the number of new abstinence pledges and a letter read from the state organization.

Then she said, "I've called you here today for one reason and one reason only." She paused for effect. "As you know, I've tried to get the council to take a vote on prohibition here in Willow Water and that didn't work—they just won't do it! Some of those councilmen want their liquor and we all know it. And most of the people don't care. Those saloons are ruining lives—we have to get the attention of the townspeople to throw them out. We have to do something drastic." Her voice dropped to its usual pitch. "I have come up with an idea." She waited for full attention, then went on, giving each word equal weight. "We will break all the windows in those three saloons!"

There was a communal gasp.

"Hilde!" Marit cried.

The ladies looked at each other in disbelief. Stella put her hand over her mouth and breathed in.

"Yes, listen, listen. We will wear our white ribbons and go as a

Hilde

group with big sticks and break all the windows in those stinking saloons."

"You've lost your mind." Nora Espeseth, a farm woman known for her good sense, stood up. "We can't do that. It's against the law to damage property. We could all go to jail."

Hilde put out her open hand. "How many jail cells are there in this town? Two." She held up two fingers and shook them. "How many beds in those cells? Two in each." She held up four fingers and shook them. "There are ten of us here." She held up the fingers of both hands and shook them.

"Count me out." Maggie Johnson, the plump town seamstress, was definite. "I will have no part in such doings."

"Wait—wait—" Hilde insisted. "Think about Ingebret Oleson. You were all outraged when we found out he died in a snowdrift just a short distance from his house—where someone left him after a drinking bout. Where did he get his liquor? I ask you."

Silence in the room.

Then Marit spoke. "But Hilde, we are a Christian organization."

"I knew you'd bring that up and I want you to remember that Christ was not always a peaceful man. He threw out the moneychangers from the temple. Right? He tipped over their tables." Hilde strode across the room miming Christ throwing tables right and left. "He scattered the money." Her square figure, her red hair helped emphasize her air of determination.

Several of the women were standing. Now others rose to their feet.

"What if the constable put a couple of us in jail—when he can't handle all of us? Hilde, have you ever seen the outhouse behind the jail? The jailer has to take the prisoners out there summer and winter."

These observations came from Mable, wife of the town lawyer. She had toured the city hall with her husband, seen the two jail cells at the back of the building, met the jailer and seen the outhouse.

Willow Water

A few women sat down as Mable spoke.

"And food. Do you know what they eat? And how do you keep clean if you're a prisoner? A woman prisoner?"

A discussion of conditions at the local jail changed the focus for a few minutes. One woman suggested there was precedence for such a project. "The WCTU has worked on prison reform, you know."

"Yes, why don't we do that?"

"Good idea."

"Let's get back to the issue here." Hilde moved around behind her chair and pounded on its wooden back. She was adamant. "If you're not willing to endure some hardship you shouldn't be in this organization."

"That's too strong a statement, Hilde," Mable protested.

"You would have us be Carrie Nations, Hilde? The WCTU never endorsed her violent actions—nor the Anti-Saloon League either." These women were well informed on their organization and the agitation for national prohibition.

Hilde put her hands on her hips. "Well, I admire her. She had courage. And she wasn't concerned about her safety or comfort."

"I think she was a little crazy," Nora interjected.

"Why don't I serve the coffee?" Stella stood to head for the kitchen.

"No, Stella," Hilde ordered. Stella sat down. "We're going to get this settled and set a time. It has to be done. We must confront the town—bring it to its senses. Can't you see that, ladies?"

"I can agree with you in principle, but not in action." Clara always knew how to say what she was thinking. "I can see you doing this, Hilde, in righteous indignation, and maybe some others here—as for me, no violence. I refuse to break windows or do anything like that."

"That leaves eight."

Maggie took Clara's hand as if to say, "Good sense is prevailing."

Hilde

"We must be united." Hilde was pleading now. "We can pay for the damage after the fact."

"What an idea!" Involuntarily, Maggie voiced her surprise.

"Will you abide by a vote, Hilde?" Marit asked her sister.

"All right then, let's take a vote." Hilde stood tall behind her chair. "How many vote to bring the alcohol problem to the attention of the town by breaking the windows in the saloons? If you vote yes, raise your hand."

No one raised a hand. There was silence. Some looked at their hands. Some looked at each other. Maggie again took Clara's hand and pressed it.

Hilde's complexion seemed to darken as she changed her tactic. "Those who will go with me stand up."

Stella Rude stood up, stiffly facing forward.

Slowly Stella's friend Agnes rose to her feet.

The rest of the women stayed seated. The room was as still as the church during silent prayer. Marit cast an anxious glance toward her frowning sister, then lowered her eyes and folded her hands.

As the women watched, Hilde gathered up her papers, picked up her purse and strode toward the door. She looked back once.

"Cowards!"

Her voice was quite clear.

Outsiders

1922-1926

"Keep your ears open at the Post Office today, Karen," Martin admonished as he struggled into his bulky winter coat.

"How so?" his wife asked as she straightened his collar.

"The word is that Pearson's building's been sold."

"Well, it's about time—that place has stood empty too long."

"Maybe someone will know who's buying and what kind of a business it'll be. I'd like to know."

Karen was one of the townspeople who gathered at the Post Office every weekday morning to wait for the daily mail. It was a kind of group ritual.

The Post Office, on a corner in the middle of downtown Willow Water, was the place one must go to pick up mail. There was no mail delivery in the town itself, only to the outlying rural area. Its main room, open to the public, contained rows of metal-fronted mailboxes on both sides of a wood-paneled middle section. A window, with a pane of frosted glass that could be opened or closed as the need arose, centered the front wall of this square-shaped area. Each morning when the bags of mail arrived the window would be closed while the Post Mistress and her assistant sorted the mail into all those metal-fronted boxes. There was sufficient room between this mid-section and the outer wall to accommodate quite a number of people, and a small crowd gathered there each day to wait for the window to open before unlocking their boxes to retrieve the contents.

Karen was not the first to enter the building that cold February morning. Conversations were already in progress as she took her usual place by one of the two large plate glass windows fronting on Main Street.

After the morning amenities she casually mentioned to the person next to her, "Martin tells me the Pearson building's been sold."

Before the window opened at ten o'clock she had found out all that the local crowd knew of this important development.

"Someone told me it's to be a shoe store."

"Naw, something to do with harnesses."

"The buyer's a man from Sweden."

"No, that's wrong, Minneapolis, I heard."

"A Swede from Minneapolis?" brought a scattering of laughter.

"I heard his name's Feinman—no, Feingold—no, that's not it either—Feinberg, that's it, Feinberg, Nels Feinberg and that he is a Jew."

Late morning of a Tuesday in March, the second week after the Feinbergs' arrival in Willow Water, Martin, his arms full of boxes,

Outsiders

struggled to open the front door of his General Store. Karen quickly moved across from her sewing supplies counter to help him.

"I met Feinberg today, Karen—at the depot."

"You did? What's he like, Martin?" Karen closed the door and followed him past the grocery section toward the back of the long building.

"Let's see—" Martin stopped momentarily to face his animated companion, "he has green eyes—" Martin sucked in his cheeks, "and purple hair."

"Martin, don't tease." Karen played with the tape measure hung about her neck.

Martin set down his load, pushed back his hair and straightened his lean, six-foot frame. "Seemed like a fine fellow to me, Karen—friendly, courteous—an intelligent sort."

"Can you tell he's a Jew?" Karen's clear blue eyes held the question.

"Well, let's see—yah, I believe he was talking Hebrew."

"Martin, you're making fun of me!" She pivoted on her heel and strode back to her domain in the dry goods section.

The Feinbergs' arrival in Willow Water was a major event, for they were the only Jews to settle in this western Minnesota, decidedly Scandinavian town.

As in every small town, new arrivals are watched and talked about. The Johansson General Store, kitty-corner across Main Street from Feinberg's building, proved to be an ideal spot for Feinberg watching. Although Martin Johansson didn't spend much time keeping an eye on activities across the street, his wife couldn't mask her curiosity. The presence of a Jewish couple in her town intrigued her. Her only knowledge of Jews came from the Bible, and what was whispered about them at the Norwegian Lutheran Church.

Willow Water

At the end of the same week, Sarah Feinberg entered the front door of Johansson's General Store looking for curtain material. Karen waited on her. The two women were about the same age, mid thirties. Karen found Sarah knowledgeable about fabrics, a bit reserved, their encounter pleasant enough, but businesslike in an almost formal way.

On the next day, a Saturday, Karen watched as Luke, the young local handyman, cleaned the windows of the Feinberg establishment—did a good job. Sarah pointed to a corner and Luke dutifully brought his cloth up to refine his work. Karen guessed that Sarah was probably a good housekeeper.

"Feinberg must have money—or one whale of a backer," surmised "Baker" Johnson on entering Johansson's. "You seen all the merchandise the dray been droppin' off there?" He stopped to look across the street before moving into the room. "His store looks real good, though—that sign ain't half bad—wha-da-ya say, Karen?" They stood together admiring the new sign across the store front above two large display windows—LEATHER GOODS—in dark red letters on a cream background, framed in forest green. "Yup, it looks real good."

Opening day for Feinberg's Leather Goods Store brought the farmers to town, and Johansson's benefited with brisk business. Ole Carlson slapped a piece of paper on the counter, "Martin, the wife's list." Martin picked up the paper and began finding the items listed while Ole carried on a monologue. "Went to Feinberg's opening today. Good stock there. Been over, Martin?"

"Haven't had time, Ole."

"That man knows harness, and him such a city slicker—all dressed up today, dark suit, shirt, tie, polished shoes even. You should see his stock, Johansson, fine harness—I could use some, if I can find the

Outsiders

cash—but," and he leaned across the counter closer to Martin and lowered his voice, "they tell me Feinberg plays the violin."

"Martin, there is a possibility that the Feinbergs will go to the Swedish Lutheran Church." Karen took off her hat, stashed it and her purse under the counter and prepared to go to work. Every other Thursday afternoon from two to four she took time off to go to the Ladies Aid program and have lunch. "I sat by Linnea Lindstrom today and she told me that the Feinbergs lived in Sweden all their lives and that they may have converted to the Swedish Lutheran Church. The Swedes are waiting to see if they come to service."

"They may have a long wait," Martin guessed.

Martin Johansson heard all the talk about the new people, was amused by his wife's compelling interest, but added nothing. In truth, he had too much to do and never time to get it all done. The arrival of the Great Northern Railroad in 1888 had brought prosperity to the community. Four grain elevators, those monoliths of the prairies, now stretched skyward above the town next to the railroad tracks. The farmers could ship their grain to the Twin Cities at a reasonable cost; their cattle could be transported cheaply as well. They began to make money and the town prospered. Martin didn't spend much of his time thinking about Nels Feinberg and his leather goods store until the late winter of 1923 when he decided to buy a riding horse. It had been his one personal desire, born of his early years on the farm, to own a fine horse for riding, and each time he carried groceries out of the store to a farmer's wagon, he circled the horses, looking them over. In talking to her friends about Martin and his love of horses, Karen would say, "He has always had a hankering for a fine riding horse of his own."

Bjornson, a horsetrader and owner of one of the livery stables in

Willow Water

Willow Water knew of Martin's interest in horses. He was sure Martin would buy a horse from him if he could just find the right one. And find one he did.

One late winter day, mounted on the back of a handsome gelding, Bjornson rode up to the front of the Johansson store, dismounted, tied the horse to a hitching post, walked across the sidewalk and through the front door to deal with Martin. In no time at all Martin became the owner of Rob, the finest horse ever seen in the farming community of Willow Water.

Martin felt like a prince riding Rob down the snow-slushy streets that memorable day and, finally, through the wide open doors of Bjornson's Livery Stable. The two men settled Rob into a stall, talked about keeping him there until spring when Martin could put him out to pasture.

Martin gave a thought to the fact that he should be hurrying back to help Karen with the business, but instead he headed for Feinberg's. At the door he hesitated a moment, then walked in to the tinkling of the warning bell. The owner, slight of build, a few years Martin's senior, came out of the back room. The two men shook hands.

"Johansson," greeted Feinberg

"Feinberg," returned Johansson.

"What can I do for you today?"

A broad grin spread across Martin's pleasant countenance. With discernible pride in his voice he replied, "I've bought a horse, Feinberg, a fine chestnut gelding and I need a saddle and a bridle, maybe a halter, too."

The next hour disappeared as the two men discussed "Horse Furnishings," as Feinberg's ad had dubbed his merchandise, Feinberg telling Johansson what was available, the different types of saddles and their appropriateness or inappropriateness for Martin's riding horse.

Outsiders

They settled on a classic English saddle with no decorations, simply good leather, well made. Feinberg didn't have one in stock, but would order the one Martin wanted right away. "It should be in Willow Water by the time spring arrives," he assured his customer.

"This is a big day for you, Johansson," observed the older man, "an auspicious occasion. I think we should have a small celebration. How about a glass of port?"

Surprised and pleased, Martin answered, "That would be good!"

Nels led Martin to the back corner of the store where a huge oak roll top desk dominated the space. He opened a deep drawer and brought out two small glasses and the bottle of wine. "Pull up." He nodded in the direction of a straight-backed wooden chair.

At least once a week through the month of March Martin would stop in at Feinberg's, ostensibly to see if the saddle and bridle had arrived. Each time they would gravitate to the corner, sit down by the big desk and begin talking. They might start discussing different leathers, collars for work horses, how to use neatsfoot oil, but invariably they would end up talking Minnesota politics or discussing national news or an article Martin had read in the *Saturday Evening Post* or some topic Nels had found in the editorial pages of the *Minneapolis Sunday Tribune*.

The friendship deepened and Martin learned about Nels and Sarah's life in Gothenburg, Sweden—how Jews had been treated in that country from the time Feinberg's great-grandfather had settled there. "We didn't leave Gothenburg because we were persecuted. We were not. We left to follow Sarah's sisters to Minneapolis in search of financial success."

While they were living in Minneapolis, Nels read a brochure put out by James J. Hill. In glowing terms the brochure laid out the advantages for businessmen to settle in the towns along Hill's Great

Willow Water

Northern Railroad in western Minnesota. Nels decided he would like to start a leather goods store in one of those towns. The growing number of farmers settling in that area could surely use harness for the horses required to work the land. Leather goods had been his stock-in-trade in Gothenburg, then in Minneapolis—why not get into this new market in northwestern Minnesota? Sarah would miss her Temple community and her sisters, but she agreed with Nels to give it a try.

The two men liked each other. They were never at a loss for topics of conversation.

"Martin, I need a few hours off one day next week. A few of us are going to call on Sarah Feinberg." Karen added new spools of green thread to a cabinet drawer as she talked to her husband.

He looked at her, lifted his eyebrows in question.

"We must start working to convert the Feinbergs."

"You what?" Martin stopped opening boxes to look directly at his wife.

"You know we've had our Mission to the Jews for years—send money to that orphanage in Jerusalem. We've been talking about it and Mrs. Swenson thinks we have a Mission to the Jews right here in Willow Water—the chance to convert two Jews to Christianity. We're going to see Sarah and invite the Feinbergs to come to an information class the minister is starting for a few people who are joining the church. We'll invite Sarah and Nels to come find out about the Norwegian Lutheran Church.

"Why, Karen, why?"

"What do you mean 'why'? Because we *should*." Karen stopped arranging the rows of thread to turn her blue eyes directly on her husband.

"Why should you?" His voice began a slow crescendo.

Outsiders

"If you ever came to church you'd know why, Martin."

The one bone of contention between the two of them had been their respective attitudes toward the Lutheran Church. Martin's rejection of the church deeply hurt his devout wife and had been the cause of many an argument in the sixteen years of their marriage. There had been tears on Karen's part and harsh words, sometimes tinged with sarcasm, from Martin. He didn't object to her bringing up their two girls in the church, but refused to take any part in it himself.

"It's our mission," Karen mumbled.

"Why can't you leave them alone? They are Jews."

"We *must* give them a chance to convert."

"Damn it, Karen, that's ridiculous!"

"Don't you swear at me, Martin Johansson." Karen closed the drawer of the thread cabinet with a bang and headed off toward the back of the store. She slammed the door as she left and he could hear her stomping up the stairs to their living quarters.

The saddle and bridle arrived in April as Nels had promised. Martin picked them up, walked down the street carrying his new horse furnishings and into the livery stable, saddled up and rode out the alley side of the building to Nels' back door. Nels, standing in the doorway anticipating his friend's arrival, came out to look at the handsome horse and its rider. He checked to see if the saddle and bridle fit properly. As he watched Martin ride off down the alley to the north and turn into the side street, he noted the easy way in which Martin settled into the saddle.

A week later the two men talked of finding a pasture for Rob now that spring was in the air. Feinberg suggested renting some pasture from Olaf Aasen up at the northeast edge of town, but Martin told him he didn't think Aasen would rent to him, that he had in mind some pastureland down by the lake.

Willow Water

In spite of Martin's opposition, Karen did go on the Mission to the Jews with Calma Storlie and Mrs. Swenson, up one flight of stairs from the Feinberg shop, to Sarah and Nels' apartment,

Mrs. Swenson, a thin woman with a needle-straight back, was the widow of a former minister of the Lutheran Church. Her husband's position in the church had given her authority, a status that she had never relinquished, and she used it to lead the women on the path she believed was Christianity. Although they had known her for twenty years, the women still addressed her as Mrs. Swenson. It was as if she did not have a first name. Calma Storlie admired the decisive Mrs. Swenson and would go along with anything she suggested. Calma was a born follower.

Late April in northwestern Minnesota can sometimes still be called winter. On this blustery spring day the women were wearing their warm winter coats, hats, gloves and even overshoes, for the streets were slushy.

When Mrs. Swenson, in the lead, opened the door at the bottom of the enclosed stairway to the upstairs rooms the cold wind entered with them. Karen, bringing up the rear, struggled to close the door. As she put her foot on the first step she was thinking, *Should we be doing this?* Martin's opposition worried her. She found herself wanting to turn around and go back home. Instead she stiffened her back and followed her companions.

At the top of the stairs Mrs. Swenson took off one woolen glove and rapped sharply on the wooden door. Sarah, her blue and white cotton housedress covered with a dark blue sweater, opened it. Although surprised to see the three women on her doorstep, she was cordial, "Do come in," she invited them, "and take off your wraps." The women took off their overshoes at the door. Sarah collected coats and hats. "I'll put these in our bedroom." When she returned the

Outsiders

ladies followed her into her front room. White lace curtains filtered the afternoon sunshine coming in the west windows.

"Make yourselves comfortable and I'll put on the kettle for some coffee."

The ladies looked around them, expecting to find some visible evidence of the Feinberg's Jewishness. Karen glanced at the books in a glass-enclosed case. The sun reflecting off the glass prevented her from reading titles. She gave a thought to Martin's love of reading and began to understand a little better his friendship with Nels. Then she noticed a violin case on the floor by a small table. She thought, *Ole Carlson is right, Nels does play the violin.* Karen began to feel ill at ease, as if she were trespassing. An uneasy silence filled the room until Sarah returned.

"I've put the kettle on to boil," she informed her visitors as she took a chair close to the kitchen door.

They talked then about sewing. Karen had sold Sarah a piece of lovely gray silk and now she asked her if she had started to work on it.

"I'm making a dress for my sister—she lives in Minneapolis—we're almost the same size so it is possible for me to sew for her. Would you like to see it?"

"Oh, yes," Karen's voice registered pleasure.

Sarah brought out the dress in progress. There was much discussion between Karen and Sarah about tucks, sleeves, the drape of the skirt. Calma and Mrs. Swenson listened as the two chattered on.

The kettle on the stove began to sing. Sarah excused herself, busied herself in the kitchen. She served them coffee in her finest china cups and passed a plate of date-filled cookies. They talked about spring, the weather and local events, until their cups were empty for a second time.

Then Mrs. Swenson set her cup on the table beside her and

Willow Water

addressed Sarah, "Our reason for visiting you today is to invite you and your husband to an information class at our church for people who want to join us."

A pregnant silence filled the sun-drenched room until Sarah spoke. "We are Jews, Mrs. Swenson, and are not at all interested in converting to Christianity—not now, not ever." Her statement was all-inclusive, final, stated firmly in a way that left no doubt.

Karen was embarrassed—she thought of Martin's question, *"Why?"* and found herself looking at Mrs. Swenson and their Mission to the Jews through Martin's eyes.

"Well, we better be going." Mrs. Swenson picked up her purse and rose from her chair. Calma, as usual, followed her lead.

Karen, to somehow ease the tension she felt, tried to draw Sarah into further discussion of the gray silk dress, "Some buttons came in the other day which might be right for the dress you are making—I remember you were looking for some and we didn't have any."

"I'll stop by and see them," Sarah agreed as she held Karen's coat for her.

The three descended the staircase in silence, closed the street door and walked half a block without saying a word.

"We tried," Mrs. Swenson stated emphatically. "The Lord will bless us. Now we must think of the biblical injunction, 'Whosoever shall not hear your words—shake the dust from your feet—and go on,' " and she reiterated, "We have tried."

After the Swedish Lutherans had waited in vain for the Feinbergs to find their way into the Swedish Lutheran Church they forgot them, became indifferent to their presence in Willow Water. Then when the ladies of The Mission to the Jews had done their duty and been rebuffed, they too simply ignored the Jewish couple in their town, didn't associate with them on any level.

Outsiders

Karen's conscience bothered her. She should invite them over for a meal because of Martin's friendship with Nels, but what would she serve them? She puzzled over Jewish food. Her desire to be accepted, in the full sense of the word, in the Lutheran Church made her hesitate about making an overture to the couple. Overcoming her husband's rejection of the church was one thing; beginning to associate with unconverted Jews was another. She did nothing.

If the Feinbergs had had children their life in Willow Water may have been different, for the social life of the town revolved around the school and the churches. As it was, they had no connections. The church people couldn't bring themselves to associate with anyone who rejected Christ. No one invited them into their homes. Everyone left them alone.

The farmers found Feinberg to be a fair businessman dealing in quality leather. They bought from him what they needed. When the townspeople planned trips, they knew where to go for a good valise, and half the inhabitants wore shoes from Feinberg's shop. Nels was busy and doing well.

As for Sarah, when the weather was nice she would slip a basket over her arm and walk out into the countryside to gather wildflowers and grasses. She found plums and chokecherries, picked them and made delicious jams and jellies. In the fall she filled her basket with hazelnuts. The women of the town saw her as she passed their houses but they never went out of their way to greet her or pass the time of day.

"I'm going to sell my business," Nels told Martin in a flat voice. The two of them were standing at the back door of Nels' store on a late-summer day.

"We've been here for four years," Nels went on slowly as Martin

Willow Water

listened. "Sarah is lonely, would like to be near her sisters, our people. The Temple. The city." He paused. The two men looked off into the distance. "We've reached the place where I can see my way clear to buy a house and move out of the apartment here on the street—the Peterson place is for sale. I wanted to show it to her." His desire to please his wife was in his voice and then he added, in disappointment, "She wouldn't go with me to see it. She's not interested in any house in Willow Water"— Nels' voice was barely audible, "wants to leave. Her feelings—are deep. She has a need to get away from here."

Martin had nodded his head from time to time in understanding.

"She wants to return to kosher food, her own people," his voice trailed off. "We're going back to Minneapolis as soon as I can find a buyer."

About Ingrid

1928-1941

Part 1

"Have you heard? Ingrid is in Bethesda." Alma lowered her voice. "A nervous breakdown."

"No! Is that so?" Marie turned and looked at her friend in disbelief.

"There seems to be no reason for it—no reason at all. The Brovolds don't know what to make of it."

Alma and Marie were sitting at the end of a long table in the basement social room of the Lutheran Church. They had come early for the Bible study because it was to be given by the minister himself.

He began, "On this day of our Lord, June 10, 1928 we are gathered here to consider . . . " He led a good study. The singing that day was thin, but adequate, and the program was over promptly at three o'clock.

Serving doors were opened and two young women moved filled plates from the counter to a serving table.

From three to five-thirty the basement hummed with feminine voices. This was their time to catch up on each other's lives and to indulge in a bit of gossip. In the vernacular of Willow Water, gossip was called "talk," as in the words of the minister's wife that day, "There's just too much talk going on about Ingrid."

And talk there was at Ladies Aid on that particular Wednesday.

A group of four women greeted Marie and Alma as they passed the table where the two were sitting. One of the four had only recently moved to Willow Water. As they settled themselves at the next table, she questioned her companions. "This Ingrid, you say she is the oldest daughter of that tall, dignified man who directed the men's chorus at the service last Sunday?"

One of the other women answered, "That's Oscar Brovold. He's the director all right, has been for years."

"I think I saw him going into the bank yesterday."

"But of course. He is the bank president!"

"Well," another of the four paused a moment before adding, "Oscar Brovold will deny this about Ingrid. No daughter of his can have a nervous disorder of any kind." And then, as if realizing she had said too much, she moved to a safer subject. "A thoughtful Bible study today, didn't you think so?"

Alma and Marie had eaten their salad and almost finished a first cup of coffee when Marie's daughter Jane joined them.

"Hello Alma." An air of exuberance surrounded the outgoing young woman. She settled herself next to her mother.

"Is it true do you think, Mother—about Ingrid? It would have made sense if this had happened when her wedding was cancelled. But that was years ago. Why a nervous breakdown now? Why now?"

About Ingrid

Alma leaned over toward Jane, shook her head and answered for Marie, "Yah—to be left at the altar that way was a hard thing to take." Alma spoke in a sing-song Norwegian brogue. "But, Ingrid, she just kept on with her work."

"She did seem to have enormous control at the time. Do you suppose she ever broke down and cried?" Marie wondered. "Maybe the reaction has been long delayed, and that's what's happening now."

"But Mother, think how long ago that was. Let's see, she left the year I graduated from high school . . ." she looked at the ceiling, "six years ago."

"Bernie hated to see her go." Marie spoke of her school administrator husband. "Ingrid was a fine teacher. And, of course, he lost Steve MacAllistair first. Steve was the best high school principal we'd had—a bad year for Bernie." She shook her head.

"That Josephine MacAllistair caused all the trouble." Alma jabbed her fork into a dill pickle. "Josephine," Alma pronounced her name with derision, "didn't want her dear boy to marry anyone. She would have made trouble, no matter what—even if he decided to marry the governor's daughter. What I'd like to know—well, a man of thirty should have a mind of his own."

"Poor Ingrid. What a shock!" Jane's imagination had been captured by the romance of Ingrid Brovold and Steve MacAllistair. Now she remembered the day of the wedding when she and her friends, after helping to decorate the church, were served tea by Ingrid's mother while Ingrid showed them some of the linens she would be using in her new home. "I wonder what she did with the things she showed us that day, the embroidered tablecloths and napkins, huck towels with pulled thread borders, pillowcases with cutwork hems."

Alma broke in, "Those Brovold women know how to do fine handwork, that's for sure. Minda may take a back seat to her important

Willow Water

husband, but she did teach her two daughters how to sew. We have to give her that."

"Her dress, Mother. Do you remember Ingrid's wedding dress?" Its high neck, the *sølje* pin she wore, and the veil with the crown of flowers. It was splendid." She rested one elbow on the table and held her face in her hand.

"Yes, Jane, I remember—Ingrid—tall and graceful."

"How could he have treated her so badly?" Jane was indignant.

While they were talking other women took places at their table and frankly listened to the conversation. Now Doris Iverson joined in, "Jane, did you see the note he sent her that night? I've always wondered what it said."

Jane turned to her questioner, "No, I did see Don bring it, but of course I didn't read it. Only Ingrid did. And then when she, *she herself*, walked up to the front of the church and made the announcement, 'There will be no wedding'—"

The women were silent for a while, re-living their quiet exodus from the church that long ago evening.

"Her announcing like that was such a Brovold thing to do," mused Doris.

"But then," a lilt entered Jane's voice, "Ingrid landed that job at St. Ansgar teaching and directing choirs. Such an honor to be at St. Ansgar!"

"There's Louise and Nora." Alma nodded toward the open door at the end of the room. The volume of talk diminished as the two women made their way toward the serving table. Louise was Ingrid's younger sister and Nora, their older cousin.

Louise and Jane had been best friends since childhood. After high school they both attended normal school in Willow Water to prepare for rural teaching, but neither had finished the two-year course. Both

About Ingrid

married before they were twenty. Nora, several years older than the two, had dropped out of high school after one year and, when she was nineteen, married the much older Ivar Hanson and moved to his farm.

As Doris watched Louise and Nora in the lunch line, she leaned over to Alma, "Ivar Hanson was sweet on Ingrid, wasn't he?"

Jane registered quiet surprise. "Nora's husband. Was he?"

"Years before the MacAllistairs came to town." Alma had lived on a farm on the shore of Willow Water Lake all her life. There wasn't much she didn't know about the community. "Yah, he wasn't the only one sweet on Ingrid. He was the only one ask her to marry him—a kinda' joke. He knew she wasn't in love with him. In the Post Office one day, when it was full of people waiting for the mail to be sorted, he walked over to Ingrid and said, loud, so everyone would hear, 'Ingrid, when are you going to marry me?' Ingrid blushed red as a beet and said, 'Oh, Ivar, quit your kidding.' "

The ladies chuckled. They liked Ivar, with his outgoing ways, his teasing.

Marie agreed, "Ivar did have an eye for Ingrid. I remember him walking her home from church choir practice. He wasn't the man for her though, a rough farmer like Ivar? I can understand her not being interested in him. Can you imagine Ingrid milking cows?"

Alma covered her mouth with her hand and whispered to Marie, "Or tumbling in the hay with him?"

Jane, not hearing Alma, asked, "Did Nora know about all this?"

Her mother was emphatic. "Of course, how could she not. Nora was in the choir, too. She saw the way Ivar looked at Ingrid. She knew he walked her home."

Nora and Louise, coffee cups and plates in hand, seated themselves at the table next to that of the talkers. Alma took her last bite of chocolate cake, finished her last drop of coffee and then turned to

Marie. "Shall we go? Can you use some eggs, Marie? My hens are laying more than we can use."

Late that afternoon Ivar Hanson came by the church to eat lunch and pick up his wife. He, too, had heard of Ingrid's illness. On the ride home he concentrated on his driving as they rode in silence around Willow Water Lake and out the county road. As they rounded the corner into their own driveway, Ivar asked, "Nora, do you think Ingrid knows about Steve's marriage?"

"Why ask me?" Nora tightened her grip on her purse and looked straight ahead. She pulled her short plump frame rigidly upright in the seat and planted her feet squarely on the floor.

"It would upset her though, if she knew, I think," Ivar speculated.

"You should know about that better than me," his wife snapped, without turning to look at him.

"Now, Nora." Ivar's voice had an edge although he meant to be conciliatory.

They stopped by the back door of the farmhouse. Nora flounced out of the car and into the house, slamming the screen door behind her.

As Ivar changed into his milking clothes he thought about his wife and Ingrid. He was the only person in Willow Water who heard from Steve. They had become good friends in the two years Steve worked at the high school. They both played basketball on the men's community team—Ivar at guard and Steve at center. The two men instinctively liked each other and their friendship extended from basketball to fishing. If Steve knew of Ivar's earlier attraction to Ingrid it did not get in the way of their friendship. Anyway, by that time Ivar had married Nora and their first son had been born.

Periodically, in the years after Steve left, a letter or a postcard

About Ingrid

marked "Portland, Oregon" would arrive in the Hanson mailbox. Ivar would read them aloud to Nora.

A few weeks before this day, in early April of 1928, he had read her a message from Steve, "Well, Ivar, I've done it. I'm married. Her name is Nancy."

Now, as Ivar pulled on his black rubber boots he was thoughtful. A picture of Nora and Ingrid flashed through his mind. It was at the Brovold family reunion a couple of years earlier. The two were standing by some high wild rose bushes up the bank by the lake. He could see the pink of the roses and hear Ingrid asking Nora, "You say Josephine MacAllistair died?" A little later he heard Ingrid say, with a slight lilt to her voice, "This will change Steve's life, won't it?" At the time, Ivar thought, *Ingrid still loves him.*

There was no sign of Nora coming to get her milking clothes. Ivar decided she wasn't coming. He would have to milk the cows alone this evening. As he opened the screen door to go to the barn he wondered—no, it couldn't be that Nora told Ingrid of Steve's marriage—she hadn't asked him to mail a letter. He shook his head and strode off across the yard toward the barn.

From Ingrid's mother Minda and her sister Louise, neighbors learned that Ingrid had made a gradual recovery from her nervous disorder and by the fall term was back at St. Ansgar. But in October Ingrid again became the topic of conversation. Louise telephoned Jane, Jane told her mother, Marie called Alma, and Alma called Doris.

There was excitement in Alma's husky voice as she asked, "Have you heard? Our Ingrid is director of the choir at St. Ansgar."

"Well, sure I know, Alma. She directs two choirs—the women's choir and the freshman choir—has been doing it for years now."

"No, no, Doris. I mean the A Cappella Choir." Alma hurried on.

71

"Eliason had a heart attack and Ingrid is the temporary director of the St. Ansgar A Cappella Choir. Can you beat that!" Alma used her favorite expression. "To be even temporary director of the A Cappella Choir is a great honor. She'll work hard at it and, who knows, she might even become permanent director."

"A woman director? Never!" Doris voiced her conviction. "There isn't a woman director in any of the Lutheran colleges in the country, not of their main choirs. It is impossible. Temporary director, sure but not *the* director."

"Ingrid could be the first." Loyal Alma's tone was hopeful.

"I can't imagine, Alma, even in my wildest dreams, that a woman could break into that all-male musical dynasty at St. Ansgar! The directorship is handed down from father to son to brother. Ingrid doesn't even have the right name. She's a Brovold, not an Eliason."

"Well, it's about time to change all that, I'd say. If she has the ability, she should have a chance at it."

"Maybe, just maybe . . ." Doris was thinking aloud, "she is there at just the right time. Eliason's only brother is an engineer and his only daughter has no musical talent at all. But never, it'll never happen."

"Let's pray for her," Alma suggested. Then she had an idea and expanded on her suggestion. "Let's all get together and pray for her."

Two months later Jane burst into her mother's kitchen. "Mother!" No answer. She raced through the hall to the stairway, grabbed the newel post and bounded up the stairs. "Mother, where are you?"

Marie met her at the top of the stairs.

"Mother, Alma was right! Alma was right! Ingrid was appointed permanent director at St. Ansgar. Louise just called and it's official. Ingrid is permanent director of the St. Ansgar A Cappella Choir!"

About Ingrid

Without thinking, Marie found herself saying, "Can you beat that!" imitating her friend Alma's sing-song voice. Mother and daughter laughed aloud as they went down the stairs together.

"Want a cup of coffee?" Marie asked as they moved through the hall into the warm kitchen. "I made cinnamon rolls this morning." She filled the teakettle with water, put it on the stove to boil, and began setting out cups and saucers.

"I'm not surprised the powers-that-be decided to make Ingrid director. It may be unprecedented to appoint a woman to the post but it is undeniable that she has the musical ability." Marie spoke with authority. "It is going to be fascinating to watch what she does. I can kind of imagine what it will do to Oscar if she succeeds."

"Mother, what do you mean by that?" Jane's voice registered surprise.

"In case you haven't noticed, Jane, Oscar is much impressed by churchmen with positions, his own in particular. What he wouldn't do to be on the board of one of the church colleges. You want half a roll?"

"A whole one, if you please. I'll get the butter. Mother, what do you think of Minda?"

Marie sat down at the kitchen table. "Minda?" She thought a while about Oscar's wife. "Minda is just there, that's all, just there."

Part 2

Ingrid raised the already well-known A Cappella Choir to new musical heights. Each spring they toured some area of the United States, even through the difficult years after the Depression. Before each tour she scheduled a concert at St. Ansgar to preview the program the choir would present that season.

Willow Water

By the spring of 1936 the businessmen of Willow Water were again beginning to prosper, Jane's husband Paul with his Ford dealership and Louise's husband Don in the insurance business. Jane suggested that the four or them take a short vacation to attend Ingrid's spring concert before the busy summer would begin.

It didn't work out. Don couldn't leave at that time, and then Jane's eight-year-old daughter Emily came down with measles so that she couldn't go either.

While Jane and Emily were housebound with the child's illness, Jane began to gather together the programs she had saved of the previous St. Ansgar concerts.

"Mama, why don't you make a scrapbook about Ingrid's choir? I'll help you. Let's do it!" Emily's enthusiasm was contagious, and Jane agreed. She began searching for newspaper clippings she had saved from the *Minneapolis Tribune* and the *Fargo Forum* about the choir's appearances.

"Do you have any letters from Ingrid, Mama? About her music—about her students—maybe about Alma's grandson?"

Jane shook her head. "No, Emily, Ingrid's too busy to write letters to me."

Yet, Jane did know that Ingrid was corresponding regularly with one person, her cousin Nora. She wondered how that correspondence had come about. Ingrid and Nora had never seemed to be at all close. It was puzzling. Now, with Emily's questioning, she remembered talking to Louise after one of the Brovold's trips to see Ingrid. Louise had told her she was surprised to hear her sister talk about Steve's work in Oregon. At the time Louise hadn't questioned Ingrid, but in telling her friend about it she had asked the question, "Jane, how did Ingrid know about what Steve was doing?" A sliver of understanding began to prick Jane's consciousness.

About Ingrid

Nora had proudly let it be known that she was receiving letters from her important cousin. People asked her in the street, "Heard from Ingrid lately?" And she would tell them the latest news. A new feeling of importance colored her life.

In her letters to Ingrid Nora would add, "Oh yes, Ivar had a card from Steve. They have moved to California." Or "P.S. Steve and Nancy are vacationing in Hawaii." Nora never allowed herself to shape into conscious thought the idea that these tidbits of information about Steve would keep the correspondence going. Yet, instinctively, since her conversation with Ingrid about the death of Josephine, she had known that by keeping Ingrid informed she would retain a favored position in her cousin's life.

When Nora and Ivar made a winter trip to the West Coast, Nora sent Ingrid a photo of herself and Ivar taken in front of the MacAllistair's spacious beachfront home. She wrote, "It seems too bad there have been no children in this big house. It would be perfect for a large family."

Nora didn't tell Ivar she had sent the photo. He didn't need to know. She did not want to discuss Ingrid with him, ever, and never spoke Ingrid's name in his presence.

"Oscar introduced another new piece tonight." Bernie settled down on the sofa next to Marie. She folded the page she was reading toward the spine of her book and closed it. "Difficult." He handed her the sheet of music. "I'll have to learn it at home so I can help the other tenors." He sat there a few moments. "Marie, have you noticed a change in Oscar lately?"

Marie shifted her position to be able to look directly at her husband. "Oscar? Well, he seems to be standing taller these days, if that's possible." She smiled. "Is that what you mean?"

Willow Water

"It's as if we are in some sort of competition," Bernie paused and looked out the window, "and there's no competition around. None of the other churches in this district have men's choruses. He's always been demanding of us, but this is different—now, he has this compelling interest in the group, bringing in new music, even scheduling practices for sections. The tenors meet tomorrow night. He's never done that before."

"I'd say Ingrid has something to do with it," offered Marie.

"You mean she's, sort of, guiding him?"

Marie shrugged her shoulders. "Well, maybe not. But Bernie, he does have to live up to his role, you know," she lifted her head and sat up straight, "as the father of Ingrid Brovold." She grinned at Bernie. "Maybe he feels he should, uh, not tarnish her reputation."

"I don't think that's it at all, Marie. He prides himself on the fact that she inherited his musicality, that he was her inspiration for choosing to go into the field of music in the first place." Marie handed the music back to him as he thoughtfully added, "Well, maybe you are right—a credit to her reputation, not his?"

He stood up, placed the sheet of music on the piano and headed for the kitchen.

Late that fall Ingrid took her choir on a European tour to the Scandinavian countries. Alma's grandson, now singing bass in the A Cappella Choir, wrote letters to his grandmother. The first one was postmarked Trondhjem, Norway. He wrote, "Grandma, you should have seen the crowd at the Trondhjem Cathedral. People were even seated in the aisles. I wish you could have been there." Letters postmarked Bergen, Oslo, Stockholm, Copenhagen, told of capacity crowds and enthusiastic audiences. Alma, exhibiting great generosity, gave his letters to Jane for her scrapbook.

About Ingrid

Saturday nights in Willow Water were special. Stores stayed open until nine, the farmers dressed up and came to town, women to do their shopping, men to pick up a few supplies and talk crops. The Main Street theater ran two films, one at 7:30, another at 9:30. Yet, for many the main event was the Saturday night band concert. The intersection of Main Street at the Post Office corner was roped off, folding chairs set up for the audience.

Alma, Doris and Marie wouldn't miss the concerts for anything. They always arrived early to get the best places to be able to see Doris' grandson in the trombone section and Alma's granddaughter in the second row of clarinets.

On a warm Saturday night in the summer of 1939 Marie arrived first carrying a lawn chair for her old friend Alma. She chose the third row back on the left side toward the middle aisle, their usual spot, and moved the metal chair to the end of the row. She had just pushed the comfortable canvas chair into place when Alma arrived.

"*Takk*, Marie, you are a life saver." Alma stuffed her shopping bag under the chair and settled her bulk into a position of comfort. She sat back and looked off into the distance.

The normally talkative group gathered in almost complete silence. Marie seated herself next to Alma. Jane approached from the other end of the aisle. As she sat down she adjusted her chair toward the group. Doris found her place and did the same, forming a kind of semicircle.

It was early, half an hour until the concert would begin. This half hour was theirs and ordinarily they would chat, enjoy the developing coolness and watch the youngsters set up for the performance.

On this night, smiles and pleasantries were missing. The atmosphere, usually lighthearted, had turned serious.

Doris looked toward Jane and asked in a hushed voice, "Do you think Ingrid will be able to conduct one of the band concerts this summer?"

"I doubt it. Louise saw her a few days ago." Jane sat silently for a few moments and then went on. "Louise was terribly upset when they returned from the city, and Minda is inconsolable. Louise told me that Ingrid barely spoke to them. She sat in the corner on the floor—Ingrid sitting on the floor! And her hair, awful, Louise said, and her dress unbuttoned."

The little group seemed to grow closer in their concern. "It must be deep depression this time," Jane continued. "The last time this happened Oscar wouldn't admit that her sickness was psychological. Remember? He simply called it 'illness' and implied a physical dimension—brought on by 'tiredness and overwork,' he would say. Remember? This time the family has been called in; he must understand how serious it is."

Doris spoke softly, "She does have a good psychiatrist, I hear."

"Yes, things are different these days—from the time she had that other breakdown—the new psychiatric wing at Bethesda and a psychiatrist instead of the family doctor."

"And this time we know what caused it." The four sat watching the gathering crowd, and then Jane added, "It seems absolutely incredible that she would carry a torch for Steve all these years. I thought surely she would find someone else."

"Maybe the last concert tour was too much for her and she would have gone into a depression anyway, without hearing of the accident." Alma wished this were true.

"No, we all know it was Steve's death caused it." Jane spoke with unusual conviction.

The young musicians were setting up their music stands, taking instruments out of cases and beginning to warm up.

About Ingrid

"Has Nora heard from her?" Alma turned to Jane.

"Not a word—since the *Chronicle* ran that article on the front page about the crash, just after it happened. I hadn't seen Nora until yesterday." She turned to her mother. "Mother, do you know what Nora said to me when I talked to her about Ingrid? She said, 'She'll recover.' That's all she said—just, 'She'll recover.' "

Doris shook her head, closed her eyes and breathed deeply. Marie took Jane's hand and held it. Alma gazed off down the street.

The band director stepped up on his box and picked up his baton. "Give us an A, David."

Part 3

There were no signs of spring in late March 1942. Winter prevailed with snow and cold winds. At a little before eight on one of those cold mornings the phone rang in Jane's kitchen. Jane's husband, at the kitchen counter sipping his hot coffee, picked up the receiver.

"Paul?" He recognized Louise's voice. They exchanged the usual greetings and then Paul handed the phone to Jane.

"Jane, I need your help." Louise's voice sounded thoughtful, not alarming as her words seemed to imply. "I can't decide what to do. Is it possible we could meet at the Meadowlark this afternoon? I don't want to be here or at your place. It's a private matter. We could sit in one of the back booths. I need to talk to someone and I know you better than anyone in town."

"Of course, Louise, I'll meet you there for coffee—what time?"

"How about two o'clock? That will give us a good two hours before school lets out." Both women had teenagers in high school. After school the Meadowlark Café would fill up with kids.

All that day Jane wondered what was bothering Louise. Could

Willow Water

Ingrid have gone off the deep end again? No, according to all reports she was doing quite well, spending a sabbatical year in Minneapolis, attending concerts, going to the theater.

Maybe it's something about her mother living alone in that big stucco house—she doesn't seem able to recover from Oscar's death. Jane thought about Minda Brovold. Thinking about Minda, as Minda, was an unusual thing to do, for Minda was seldom considered for herself. She had spent her life in the shadow of her important husband, her famous daughter and yes, even of Louise. Jane remembered a conversation she'd heard between her mother and Minda. They were discussing a move that some friends of theirs had made to Chicago and Minda had said, "I wouldn't move to a city ever. It's much better to be a big fish in a little pond than to get lost as a little fish in a big pond." At the time Jane had been impressed with the fact that Minda had come up with a metaphor.

Jane thought of Louise—calm, competent Louise, the only woman she knew who hadn't a selfish cell in her body. In fact, people took advantage of her competence and her generosity. Jane realized that she felt sorry for Louise. Louise, who had always carried the troubles of the whole Brovold family on her slim shoulders: Ingrid's depressions, Oscar's death last year. And now she was trying to settle Oscar's business affairs and take care of her ailing mother.

Minda, at 69, was unable to function without her domineering husband. Jane had begun to think that Alma was right when she prophesied at the time of his death, "Without Oscar, Minda won't last long."

Jane barely noticed what she was doing with her hands, making beds, doing laundry, washing dishes. She wondered if the Brovolds realized the role Louise played in their lives, if they were ever concerned about her. *Did Ingrid ever give a thought to Louise? Maybe Louise and Don*—no, she rejected the idea, impossible. They have a good marriage.

About Ingrid

Paul had gone out of town, wouldn't be home for the noon meal. She ate a sandwich by herself at the kitchen table and gazed out at the snow-covered yard. Her thoughts wandered. *How would Mother handle it if Dad died?* She answered her own question, *She'd be all right, she would go on, make a life for herself.*

Finally, *enough of this*, she told herself. She turned on the radio and walked into the bedroom to change her clothes.

Several local men were drinking coffee at the counter and two strangers were seated in a front booth as Jane and Louise entered the café. They chose the next-to-the-last booth on the south side of the room, out of earshot of customers or kitchen help.

"Hello, Dorothy," Louise greeted the waitress who set two glasses of water on the table. Jane smiled at her.

"What kind of pie has Edna baked today?"

"There's the usual apple, and sour cream raisin and lemon meringue."

The two women placed their orders and Dorothy left to fill them.

"I've been thinking about you all day, Louise. What is this all about?"

"I don't mean to be so mysterious, Jane, but I've found some things that bother me. I've been going through Father's papers, trying to get everything in order. I wish Ingrid would help me, but I hesitate to ask her to come up here, with Mother the way she is. She's enjoying her sabbatical and I don't want to worry her."

Dorothy brought coffee, cream and sugar. Louise added cream to her coffee without losing the train of her thought. "Trying to sort things out takes so much time. I spend hours. Father left a disorderly mess. He deteriorated last year when he was nearing his eightieth birthday. Everything is mixed up. I found his appointment books."

She paused. "They make interesting reading, to say the least. Father never told us about his dealings at the bank. I'm learning of financial matters that are changing the way I view people I know—and I'm wondering about my father. His assessment of the men and women he would see, short statements, his judgment of character—some quite unbelievable. We never really know our parents, do we?" She looked up from stirring her coffee, way off, as if into the far distance. "Father seems to have preferred dealing with his church friends. He refused loans to those he didn't like or whose religion didn't measure up. And I thought . . ." She let her sentence dangle there.

Dorothy approached carrying a dessert plate in each hand. "Two pieces of sour cream raisin," she announced. "I'll be back with more coffee."

Jane picked up her fork but neither of them started to eat.

"In Father's papers I found a letter addressed to him from the financial officer at St. Ansgar. It's dated April 20, 1922."

" The year of Ingrid's wedding." Jane put down her fork.

"The no-wedding," corrected Louise. "Well, the letter was about financial aid for a student at St. Ansgar, a Willow Water boy getting financial aid. But the last paragraph is about Ingrid. The financial officer wrote —let's see if I can quote it. 'We at St. Ansgar have heard very good reports of your daughter's high school choir in Willow Water, in fact, Eliason was one of the judges for the state music contest last year and was mightily impressed with her choir's performance.' It went something like that."

Jane interrupted, "The year they won the first?"

"Yes, it was. Then he said that the director of the women's choir was moving on and there would be a vacancy in the music department. He said he was sure Ingrid could take her place, if she chose to and finished with, 'Why don't you ask her to get in touch with Eliason.' "

About Ingrid

The enormity of what Louise was saying began to penetrate Jane's consciousness. "But, Louise, what are you thinking?"

"You know Father's high regard for Eliason, for the music of the church," her voice dropped, "and his own reputation."

"But, Louise, would he—do you think he told Ingrid about this before the wedding?"

"No, I don't think so. I'm sure he didn't."

"Then you're wondering who he did tell, right? Or if he told anyone?"

"Listen, Jane, there's more. As I was looking through Father's appointment book for 1922 I found that Josephine MacAllistair had appointments with Father three times during April and May of that year. She was in financial trouble—lost a pile of money on an investment she made after her husband died. Father approved a big loan for her."

"Are you thinking the two of them . . ."

"She'd made it clear she didn't want Steve to marry Ingrid. Everyone knew that. There was some doubt she would even attend the wedding. She didn't think Ingrid was the right person for her Steve—I'm afraid of my suspicions, Jane. Would Father do this? Go this far? Be underhanded? Status in the church was so important to him. After Ingrid made it to the top at St. Ansgar, he was extremely proud of being Ingrid's father. It gave him a position. . ." Louise didn't finish that thought, "and later he was appointed to the board of the college. You did know that, didn't you, Jane?"

Jane nodded. "Do you think your mother knows anything about all this?"

"I'm sure she doesn't. Father never discussed bank business with Mother. She had no idea what he did at the bank. And she isn't the least intuitive, never has been."

Dorothy came by with more coffee.

Louise went on, "If Josephine told Steve about Ingrid's chance to go to St. Ansgar, would Steve have?—No, I don't think so, he was not, surely he wouldn't—but then, she could have implored him not to marry Ingrid—to assure that Oscar Brovold would okay the big loan she needed."

"That puts a different light on what happened," Jane stated. "And on the character of Steve."

"And my father." Louise looked down at the table.

They were quiet. Louise took a bite of her pie. "I could be wrong about all this, couldn't I, Jane?"

"That's possible, Louise."

"*Was* Ingrid just not the woman for Steve, as Josephine insisted?" Louise questioned. "Their engagement was such a formal thing," Louise looked at Jane, "the very opposite of your tempestuous love affair with Paul."

Jane lifted her head, closed her eyes, sat back and took a deep breath.

"Is it possible Steve wanted out before his mother got involved? Maybe he was having second thoughts—not very kind of me, is it, Jane?" Louise was bothered by the trend of her thoughts.

"When he was killed, why did it throw her the way it did?" Jane asked.

"Maybe the what-ifs began to plague her. What if I had not done this, what if I had not been that way?"

"She never really experienced failure, except with Steve. Louise, what if she had married Steve—and lived here all her life, like we are doing?"

"She would have had kids, maybe quit teaching."

She'd probably be directing the church choir now.-"

About Ingrid

"And singing solos for weddings and funerals."

They both half-smiled.

"How do you think Ingrid will take it if you tell her?" Jane finally asked the important question.

"I've thought about it and thought about it."

"And the thing we're both considering, will she go into a depression again, or on the other hand, would it be freeing and would she finally get over the whole thing?" Jane suggested.

"Maybe she is over it." Louise let the possibility hang there.

The two were so intent on their conversation that they had not noticed the high school kids milling around the front door. Dorothy had removed their plates. Their cups were empty.

Jane reached across the table and took both of Louise's hands in hers. They sat there for a second. "Louise, I can't tell you what to do. You have to decide." She rose slightly, leaned across the table and gave Louise a kiss on the cheek.

Louise looked into her friend's eyes. "Dear Jane, I knew that would be what you would say." Louise was sitting with her back to the front of the café and didn't see her son starting down the aisle toward them. She went on, "But I had to talk to someone, to someone who would listen." She dropped her head to their clasped hands.

Embarrassed by their public display of affection, her son turned around and joined the young crowd at the door.

Springtime Rebellion

1968

The day began as usual. A rooster crowed. Birds began to twitter in the trees. Marit heard these outside sounds through the open window. Hilda had always said, "Leave the window open one inch, at least. A little fresh air is good for you." *Hilda knew what was good for you. She was a nurse. She always told you what was good for you and she expected you to listen and heed her words.* Marit thought of Hilda— *Hilda was solidly built, like the Hanson side of the family, stocky, square, strong. Ole laughed and said that Hilda was so strong—no, tough, he said, that she would live forever. But she died, like everyone else. Only the weak live to be eighty-nine, like me,* she decided. Marit smiled to herself. There was no one else to smile at. She was alone—in the big square house. The big, square house was quiet, so quiet. Sometimes she thought she heard one of her brothers upstairs. *They must be gone,* she thought. *Oh, they've been gone for years!* The sun came up and touched the flowered wallpaper; a spray of lilacs bloomed in the warm light. Marit looked at the calendar hanging on the back of the closed door. *You don't hang calendars on the walls, you know, but you can hang one behind the door. No one will see it.* She felt a satisfaction at having a calendar with big numbers, from the bank, big black numbers, easily seen. *It's April. Twenty-ninth? Thirtieth? Oh well, it doesn't matter. It's April.* Marit liked April. She could hear the wind soughing through the pines. In northwestern Minnesota spring can be blustery. *The wind—maybe it is March and I turned the calendar page too soon. No matter.* "Marit!" She thought she heard Hilda call her name. "Nothing gets done if you stay in bed all day," Hilda had always said. Marit did not move. *Hilda is not here. She died—in February? She didn't call me—it's just my imagination.* Marit thought about force of habit, about getting up when you are called.

She turned over and looked out the south window. *Maybe Halvdan is out there mowing. Now Marit,* she chided herself, *if this is April there is no hay to mow. I like Halvdan. He is so steady. If I had married I would have married someone like Halvdan. What if I had married?* She looked at the ceiling and imagined herself married to Halvdan. *I would have moved to a different place—instead of spending eighty-three years on this one.* Irritation brought action and Marit sat up, lowered her thin feet to the floor and into her waiting slippers.

The morning routine slowly unfolded. The sun was well up in the sky before Marit sat down at the kitchen table for breakfast. She and Hilda had breakfasted together in that dark north kitchen for—always, it seemed. Marit had suggested they move to the dining room on the south side of the house, set up a little table right by the bay window and look at the geraniums as they ate. "That takes too much time. Dallying over breakfast is a bad habit to get into." Marit picked up

Springtime Rebellion

her bowl of cereal, walked into the sunny dining room, pulled a chair over to the bay window and gloried in the salmon color of the geraniums.

Is this the day the Circle is coming for coffee? Hilda always arranged things, made the plans, assigned tasks. *If we are having Circle,* thought Marit, *I must get ready. Find the tablecloth, the Hardanger one. I hope it is clean and ironed,* she worried. Hilda always said, "We use the best for the church." Hilda would have bustled around. Marit could almost see her getting out the silver service from the corner cupboard. "What's the use of having it if we don't use it?" Hilda, who prided herself on frugality, had tried to justify this touch of ostentation. Marit thought, *Hilda maybe secretly liked being better than the other ladies, having a silver service and using it for Circle. Oh no, that is an ungenerous thought.* Marit heard the imperious voice, "You must clean the silver service while I drive into town for groceries." She sat by the bay window, forgot Circle, forgot Hilda, forgot the silver service, enjoyed the sunlight on the bright blossoms. The sun climbed higher in the sky.

The phone rang. Marit ignored it. It rang again. She sighed and slowly walked through the kitchen into the wide front hall. It was her niece. Yes, she was fine this morning. No, it didn't matter if Jen didn't come by today. She needed nothing. Yes, yes, she was in good spirits. She placed the phone into its cradle and sat there, looking out the etched glass of the front door. *It's close in here,* she thought, feeling a touch of claustrophobia. *Should I open the door? Hilda wouldn't like that—letting out the heat.* She opened a drawer and found the key to the door. "We'll keep the front door locked," Hilda had said, "just to be safe." *Who will come in? I have no enemies. Did Hilda have enemies?* She fumbled with the lock. Perhaps she should find the doorstop and leave it only slightly ajar. Not finding the needlepoint-covered brick behind the door, she forgot it and flung the door wide open. The cool spring air rushed in. *Ahhhhhhhh, it smells so good.*

If we are to have Circle, the thought was an anxiety, *I must polish the coffeepot and the teapot, the creamer and the sugar bowl. Maybe the coffeepot is enough, nobody takes tea—except Mrs. Swenson.* Marit moved into the living room. The mahogany piano on the west wall was flooded with the morning sunlight streaming in from the bank of south windows. Marit sat down on the stool. It was too high. She stood and twirled the top clockwise, then seated herself again. On the rack in front of her the old hymnal lay flat and open to "Children of the Heavenly Father." *Page 273,* she noted. *How many times have I said, "Children, turn to page 273. Here is your pitch—sopranos, altos."* She took the hymnal from the rack and turned slowly around. She seemed to see in front of her two rows of faces. Together they started to sing. "Children of the Heavenly Father, safely in His bosom gather." Marit beat time with her book, moving it up and down in rhythm. She dropped the book to her lap. *All those children. How many years? Thirty? Forty? The children had children.* Names began returning to her—Scandinavian names mostly. She spoke them aloud, giving them their Norwegian pronunciation. "Hjordis, Gudrun, Helga, Eric, Karen, Beret, Harald." The children, the children. "Marit!" Hilda always said, "save the practicing until evening, after the sun goes down. In the daytime we work." Marit replaced the book on the piano and started to get up, thought better of it, moved the hymnbook and found a thin, faded yellow volume from the stack of music on a chair near the instrument. She paged through until she found the piece she wanted. *Mozart, I love Mozart.* Her fingers were stiff but she took pleasure in her playing. The sun reached its zenith.

Oh yes, the silver. She rose, went into the dining room to the corner cupboard, found the tray, the coffeepot, the teapot, the creamer and the sugar bowl. She decided to polish them on the dining room table

Springtime Rebellion

and set about spreading newspaper over the oak top. *Before I start I'll have a glass of milk.* "You must eat a nourishing meal, Marit. If I'm not here you must take the initiative and make a nourishing meal." *Hilda was so bossy. I don't feel like eating—just milk.* Again she chose to sit by the flower-filled window.

A robin hopped across the lawn. *On a nice day like this a little walk would be just the thing. But Circle, the silver. Maybe I can take it with me and sit down there by the river while I polish it—and use water from the river to rinse it. A good idea!* She hurriedly found her coat and scarf. As she lifted the tray she found it an awkward thing to carry. She needed something to carry it in—*a gunnysack. There's a gunnysack on the back porch.* She found it, put the silver into it, all the silver. The sack was too heavy. She removed the teapot, set it way back in the corner cupboard behind a stack of plates, *where Hilda won't see it. There, that's better. I will go out the back door and across the pasture to the river. It's not far.* When she opened the back door the wide open front door allowed a veritable gale to sweep through the house. She struggled to close the door. *Outside! To feel the sun and the wind! Not to be inside! And the grass is turning green.* She made her way around the weathered barn and struck off across the pasture. The ground was wet. Marit reminded herself that she should have worn her overshoes, but she didn't want to go back.

Down by the river a clump of spring green willows beckoned. *The cowslips are in bloom—what a bright, cheerful yellow. I'm glad I came.* A cow mooed off in the distance. In a few minutes she was as close to the stream as she could get, for the banks were muddy. She found a downed tree, dropped her load and sat down. Then a clear conception of time came to her. *It must be one o'clock or later. And Circle at two thirty. I should not have come. What will Hilda think of me! Well, I better get at the silver.* She opened the sack. No silver

Willow Water

polish. No rag. Sometimes Hilda had said, "Marit, you are thoughtless." She conceded, *I am thoughtless.*

Sitting on the log in the bright sunshine, she felt warm. The wind had diminished to a soft caress. As she took off her scarf one of the hairpins that held her braids caught in the knitted blue wool. She began to take out all the pins. The severe braids, which had encircled her head, fell to her shoulders. She shook them out, running her fingers through them as she did when she prepared to wash her hair. *How comfortable with no pins. Maybe I should have my hair cut short.*

With no polish to clean the silver, she would have to carry it back, tarnished yet. *Oh no, I can't do that!* She took the ornate coffeepot out of the sack. Idly her fingers traced the pattern on its side. *Mother liked her silver—it was a link to the old country for her.* She lifted the cover and looked in. Then she set it on the log on which she was sitting. It fell off and rolled over near her feet. She took out the creamer. Its feet were especially dark. *They need work,* she noted. *It's so hard to get those feet clean.* She felt the burden of tasks. *To be free of tasks!* She stood up————and then————she did an unthinkable thing! She hurled the silver creamer as far as she could toward the river. It splashed into the water just beyond the willows. The sugar bowl met the same fate.

Marit found the action exhilarating, and the tray sailed through the air much farther than Marit thought she could throw it, way into the middle of the stream, glinting in the sunlight as it flew. Only the coffeepot was left at her feet. *It, too, might as well go.* She tossed it after its companions. It fell short of the river and landed upright in the mud along the bank. Marit picked up the gunnysack, started to fold it neatly, changed her mind, and wadded it into a ball. Just as she tossed it up into the air the wind picked up and caught it, carrying it downstream until it fell in and floated on the water.

Springtime Rebellion

The breeze suddenly felt cool. She buttoned her coat, turned and headed back across the pasture toward the barn and the house. She walked easily, gracefully, feeling light and free. The fragment of a hymn came into her mind, *nothing in my hands I bring, nothing in my hands I bring.* She held out her slender blue-veined hands. The west wind blew her loose white hair back from her face. The sun shone and a meadowlark sang—just for her.

Photograph by Ruby Williams

Jean Vaatveit Husby grew up in the farming community of McIntosh in Northwestern Minnesota where its Scandinavian people, who perpetuated their old-country traditions, made an indelible impression on her life. After she married she lived in Kansas City, Missouri, where she helped raise a family, began to write stories, worked as a musician and earned a university degree. She now lives, with her husband Harold, on Maple Hill within sight of Lake Superior at Grand Marais.

Scott Husby has been a hand bookbinder since the early 70s and was introduced to wood engraving by a friend in 1995. He is currently Conservator for Rare Books at Princeton University.

NORMANDALE COMMUNITY COLLEGE
LIBRARY
9700 FRANCE AVENUE SOUTH
BLOOMINGTON, MN 55431-4399